For Billy— To va[...]
[...]twelve [...]
Much magic, many
adventures to you!

Runie Munson
December, 1974

A Fistful of Sun

A Fistful of Sun

by Tunie Munson

illustrated by Richard Cuffari

Lothrop, Lee & Shepard Co. / New York

1 2 3 4 5 78 77 76 75 74

Library of Congress Cataloging in Publication Data

Munson, Tunie.
  A fistful of sun.

    SUMMARY: Newly moved to the country, a lonely city girl finds solace in a barn loft where an equally lonely boy raises pigeons.
    [1. Friendship—Fiction. 2. Pigeons—Fiction]
I. Cuffari, Richard (date) illus. II. Title
PZ7.M928Fi   [Fic]   74-6420
ISBN 0-688-41647-0
ISBN 0-688-51647-5 (lib. bdg.)

For my mother and my father who gave the magic,
For Ken who shared it,
And for Peter who lets me go on believing in it.

1.

What can you do with an empty room and miles of sky beyond you? Jennifer stretched her fingers and reached for a piece of the sun. At the moment her fingertips reached for the sky, Jennifer saw the crinkled wad in a corner of the attic window. A small piece of paper, folded and folded again, and jammed between glass and window frame. It seemed strange that she had not noticed it before.

"The day we moved in, when we listened to the rain—why not then?" she wondered.

The first day she and her mother and father had moved to Del Norte, a month before, they had climbed the staircase up past the bedrooms into the empty room beneath the roof. The shape of it had reminded Jennifer of the arts and crafts room on Gilpin Street in Denver, where she had spent her Tuesdays with Lisa and Gerard, her friends.

"I love the peace of this place," her father had said as they had listened to the rain beating against the attic roof, inches from their heads. "The rat race in Denver was getting me down. No happiness there."

7.

"Just crowds and noise," her mother had replied, and smiled now that they were away from it all.

If they had asked Jennifer for her opinion, she would have told them that she hadn't minded the crowds, especially those in the park on Sundays. She would have added that she had rather enjoyed the noise of the street sweeper and the sound of traffic in the street below her window. And the cry of the burrito vendor whenever a passerby eyed his meat sandwiches, "Boooreeetohss!"

"It's good to be alone," her father had sighed, content.

It's good to be alone. His words came to Jennifer's mind again and again. She had watched him walk to the small patch of corn beyond the aspen and to the vegetable garden behind the house, strolling aimlessly. Often in the late afternoon he left his workroom to search, he said, for a sunset. He was happy here, that was certain.

Just yesterday, without the slightest warning he had twirled Jennifer in the air the way he had done when she was five or six; he had stretched an arm out and said, "What say we grab a fistful of sun, Jen?"

A rather strange thing for her father to say. One day he had been all hurry, grabbing his briefcase and gulping his coffee on the run with hardly a goodbye for anyone. And today—every day since the first in July—he had been doing different things like grabbing for a piece of sunshine. A very strange development, Jennifer thought.

Yet, the memory had prompted a try, and, reaching for the sun, she had found this hidden message.

8.

"Beanbrain!" Jennifer thought. "Who says this has to be a message? The paper could have been tucked in to keep away drafts."

Jennifer pulled the wad of paper from its hiding place. No, it was definitely too small to keep out breezes and winter air.

She sank down on her knees to unfold it. If only the paper held a mystery or some exciting secret . . . then she might not miss so much the burrito man and the room on Gilpin Street and the Sundays in the park. Then the days might not be so empty.

Yes! Jennifer could see ink markings on the paper. Jennifer closed her eyes to imagine the message before the final unfolding:

Help! I am about to be imprisoned in the cellar
for life with no hope of ever escaping.

Or perhaps it was a warning:

Beware: this house is haunted.
Get out while you can!

The room seemed darker and bigger as Jennifer opened her eyes. Another message appeared in the air before her:

I, Henry Thatcher, killed five people in this
room. This very moment I am lurking behind
you and you will be my next victim.

Jennifer jumped up and dashed for the door, scrambling down the stairs. In the sunlight of her bedroom, she felt rather ridiculous. Fortunately, no one had been around to witness her flight. Jennifer eyed the message again.

9.

"A note," she decided to herself. "That's what it will be. Something like, 'Horace, don't forget to buy some rhubarb.'"

She could no longer stand the suspense. She unfolded the paper and there, in her hands, were the penned words:

MAGIC IN MY LOFT, SPECIAL MAGIC

Jennifer had to read it again to let the words sink in. "'My loft' . . . hmmm. Only one loft around here," she thought. "And there's nothing magic about it."

Jennifer climbed the dark stairway winding up to the attic. She stopped at the door in spite of herself to check for Henry Thatcher, and then crept to the window. From the single window, the hayloft of the barn on a slope of land beyond the trees was barely visible.

The window was a high one. The panes of glass were full of clouds and blue. In the lowest corner, the top of the barn bit a hunk from the sky. The roof of the barn was patched and worn. Under the eaves was the loft opening. Jennifer had explored the floor of the empty barn. No magic there, she was certain. She read the note again, slowly:

MAGIC IN MY LOFT, SPECIAL MAGIC

"Why would anyone cram those words behind a window frame?" Jennifer wondered.

The letters were cramped and scribbly, as if a little child or someone very old had scrawled the words. Someone playing practical jokes or dreaming silly dreams.

10.

Jennifer didn't believe much in magic, certainly not the rabbit-in-the-hat kind, and lately, not other kinds either. More than once in the city, when the moon at her window had been of a special brightness, she had watched the night sky, moving beyond her understanding, holding the secrets of time and space, and had wished on the stars. There had been times when she had felt the magic—felt as if anything wonderful, surprising, might happen if only people would believe.

Had she been crazy to believe that wishes come true? No, it was her parents who had gone crazy, buying a piece of land in the middle of nowhere. Couldn't they see that no amount of wide open spaces could make up for having to leave her friends? And didn't they know that it was as easy to be alone in the crowds of the park on Sundays as in any vegetable patch? But her parents had somehow clung to the notion that back-to-nature meant instant happiness, and Jennifer had felt powerless to change their thinking. The stars had not helped either.

The last night in her city room, Jennifer had stayed at the window, willing time to stop, to go backward; wanting a way to escape from the moving and the growing up alone. But the stars, burning far away, had faded into morning. And the magic, not strong enough to juggle time, had gone. No longer, she had decided, would she believe in it.

There could be no magic in an empty loft. Yet, Jennifer found herself making her way down the stairway, skipping over the lawn and through the stand of aspen hiding the old barn. With the building in sight, she raced between two rows of corn, already grown above her head, to stand before the tumbledown barn. By the time she reached the doorway she was very much out of breath. She pulled back her head and gazed straight up at the loft opening, a big yawn in the high wooden wall.

Jennifer walked into the dark cave of the barn, feeling the heat around her. The strong sweet smell of hay made her crinkle her nose. It was so quiet that she could hear her own breathing and the flutter of wings above her.

2.

The ladder to the loft was there, rickety, narrow, nailed to the loft floor. Jennifer imagined a top rung breaking beneath her feet to send her tumbling through the air to the ground. She tested the bottom rungs with her fist, pounding each as hard as she could. One wobbled, another creaked. None broke.

The ladder moved up through a hole in the wooden floor of the loft. It was a large hole, a square actually, giving a glimpse of hay and light far above her.

Jennifer began the climb, rung by rung, groping her way up toward the last step. Her knuckles were white with the grasping.

"How long would it take them to find me if I fell?" she wondered. "Too bad Gerard isn't here for pointers."

Gerard could climb any fire escape and would certainly have known how to tackle a loft ladder. Bringing Gerard to mind helped her forget the dizzying height. When she reached the top, she paused to look around before the final scramble through the opening.

The roofbeams soared high above her. Touching the lower ends of the beams and hiding the walls of the loft were bales of hay. The hay was all around her, in big blocks, tied and stacked in towering shapes. The odor and the warmth made Jennifer feel as if she'd come upon a strange living being.

"Like a beast, a friendly one," she thought.

Clenching the sides of the ladder, she glanced at the floor below. The ladder appeared to get smaller, narrowing as it reached for the ground. It formed a "V" from top to bottom. She fought her yearning to climb, slow and easy, back down.

Loosing her hold of the ladder, she leaned over the top of it and pressed her palms to the loft floor. Her hands, clawing, advancing, helped to pull the rest of her body over the last rung to the floor. On the solid flooring, she quickly crawled away to lie back against the hay, an unbroken wall of it soaring toward the ceiling.

A narrow path ran from one end of the loft to the other, where a jumble of bales lay like giant building blocks tumbled from a golden skyscraper. Bits of hay and feathers, grit and pebbles brushed the planks.

Jennifer imagined all kinds of uses for the blocks at the end of the barn loft. . . . They might be moved and turned on end and arranged into igloos and hotels with

13.

corridors of rooms and split-level houses and three-story castles. As Jennifer caught her breath and studied the hay, she became aware of sounds somewhere near her. She was not alone.

To be sure, they were peaceful sounds that reached her ears—squeaks and coos and grunts, whistles and, every now and then, a whoosh through the air.

Jennifer inched curiously along the few yards of planking that led toward the murmurs coming from the center of the loft. She noticed that ahead of her there was an opening in the hay—a wide patch of floor between two towers of hay. Jennifer hesitated, then stepped out into the open patch of floor, amazed, astonished by the sight. She faced the wooden wall of the barn, graced by a doorway open to the sky, and above her, around her, gliding over the threshold toward her, soaring out into the air, were pigeons—and more pigeons!

They were perched in the rafters and nestling atop the hay on each side of her. Others were pecking at the floor or fluttering to and from the loft door. Motionless, speechless, she watched them.

Oh, she had known pigeons all right. They perched on the hats and guns of the statues in the park. They bothered the bench people for popcorn and bread crumbs. They congregated on the park walks and on apartment sills and they left droppings as reminders of their visits.

Jennifer had preferred the tiny sparrows, leaving the pigeons to the old folks on the benches with their bags of bread. But these birds were different, lovelier,

14.

prouder somehow than their relatives in the city. Finding them in their home, the loft, in pockets of hay and on dark heavy beams, was like finding a secret— or like seeing something old in a new way, in such a way as to take one's breath away.

The big wide doorway made everything else more beautiful. The golden hay, trying to touch the ceiling, flanked the entry. The heavy door of weathered wood, hung together by an "X" of planks, drifted out to the sky with each gust of wind, then back to the birds.

Moving past the doorway were creampuff clouds in a blue bowl of sky. The smell of pine, cool and green, and a wind from the mountains filled the space at the door. Jennifer watched the birds flutter out of the opening, becoming a part of the sky. Jennifer wished she could follow them.

"How special to be born with wings," she thought.

Wings, for one thing, would make the trip down from the loft much easier. Remembering Gerard, she recalled the time, on their way down a fire escape, they had glimpsed a man crooning and grinning in his bubble bath.

The quiet of the loft invited remembering. Remembering the funny way Lisa could wrinkle her nose, pushing the freckles into bunches . . . the taste of burritos from the old man's cart, the chili and cheese melting in the mouth . . . the way sidewalks sounded under roller skates . . . a suddenly bashful Lisa, on moving day, offering Jennifer an arrowhead, her best, before they had hugged goodbye.

With the remembering a wave of emptiness washed

over her, sweeping thoughts away and leaving her small and still and lonely.

Willing away the remembering, Jennifer turned to the pigeons resting in pockets in the hay. Someone had made the pockets for them, scooping from the bales handfuls of hay. Several birds peered from their shadowy shelters, studying Jennifer.

"Don't worry. I won't hurt you," she assured them. "I won't wreck your homes."

Where could she build her kingdom of hay, without disturbing the pigeons? She remembered the jumble of hay at the end of the barn loft and hurried to the pile.

The bales were bulky cubes, tied with heavy twine. Many had toppled to the floor, making of the remaining tower a kind of staircase rising to the roofbeams.

Jennifer scrambled up and over the makeshift steps, heading back toward the wall of pigeon pockets. Half-way up the make-believe mountain, a wall away from the pigeons, she confronted a bale tilted on end and another perched precariously behind it, waiting to tumble. Jennifer pulled the first out and into the air, watching it career down to the loft floor, lodging against the pile of hay below. She pressed a shoulder against the second, nudging it over, out of her way. It fell away easily and left, in full view, a tunnel-like opening.

Jennifer peered into the hole; it extended the length of several bales of hay and ended at the barn wall, where a glimmer of light beckoned. She squeezed into the tunnel, making her way through the burrow in the warm tickly hay. She felt like a worm wriggling its way to sunlight.

The tunnel opened into a space where the sloping roof met the wooden wall. Jennifer reached up and touched a roofbeam above her head—a good feeling to be tall enough to touch a rooftop. City ceilings had always been beyond her reach.

She saw that three of the walls and the floor of the space were made of hay. The fourth was the wooden wall of the barn. Through cracks and chinks in the planks, it welcomed bits of sunshine and breeze. And in the corner was a tiny window shining with light. Four frames of glass filtered the sunlight through a film of dust. The shafts of wavering light shone with millions of dust particles, giving to the Jennifer-sized room a strange luminescence.

She rested, happy and proud of her discovery, listening to the birds a few feet away on the other side of the hay. Then she scooted to the window.

Her finger followed the groove around the frame and found the latch. Jennifer saw that it was rusty and worn, but soon it gave way to her tugging. After a few firm pushes, the old window creaked open to let in the sky. Jennifer poked her head out, drinking in the blue. Her heart pounded as she took in the view.

The house and the aspen grove were small enough to clutch in her hand. Far away a mist of clouds skimmed the edges of the mountaintops. She saw the land as a bird might see it; indeed, she felt like one as her gaze moved over the earth.

17.

Jennifer's mother, seeming like an elf of a person from this height, appeared on the porch. She called Jennifer to supper. Jennifer ducked from sight, though she doubted her mother would think to look for her under the roof of the barn.

She wriggled through the tunnel. She waved a good-bye to the birds. Then, with much scuffling and praying and clutching, she backed from the ledge to dangle one foot into the air. Her foot felt for a rung. She waited for the other to do the same. Eyes closed, Jennifer worked her way down to the barn floor to a sigh of victory and relief.

She hurried outside, around the corner of the barn, and looked up at the loft, up at the big doorway and at the little window she had never even noticed before today.

She had never had a secret hiding place before— not one that Gerard or Lisa had not eventually found. And what a place it was! She had been a bird in that place. Nothing could reach her there.

"It's good to be alone," Jennifer said to the sky and the trees.

She wondered if it would be good tomorrow, this being alone. It did not matter. At last, if only for today, she had said the words and believed the belief of her father. Today, alone was enough.

20.

3.

After supper, Jennifer's mother made the announce-
ment. It came as Jennifer was sneaking past the sink
and the supper dishes. She had almost reached the door
when her mother tossed her a dishtowel.

"Aunt Bertha is coming."

Her mother said it as simply as if she had only given
the temperature. For a moment, Jennifer stared at the
towel. She tried for words, but none would come.

She settled for something between a scream and a
groan. It sounded terrible. It fit the occasion. Jennifer
would have continued to improve upon it if her father,
absorbed in cleaning crumbs from the tabletop, had not
beat his fist on the table for silence.

Jennifer stuffed the dishtowel in her mouth and continued a silent scream. As the weight of the news hit
her smack in the chest, she squinted her eyes and gave
her parents an ugly stare. She remembered to remove
the towel before she spoke.

"You've already invited her to visit us here? How
could you?"

"We had to," her father said. "She needs a place to
stay while her landlord remodels the apartment. They'll

21.

tear up the kitchen, the bathroom . . ." He tucked the placemats into a drawer and headed upstairs. "We can't expect Bertha to live there through all that."

Jennifer yelled after him. "We can't expect me to live through a visit from Aunt Bertha!"

Her mother gave the kind of sigh that showed she was vexed, that Jennifer was making something out of nothing.

"Jennifer, act your age!"

Those words were her mother's answer to everything. Those words were supposed to end any conversation. Jennifer had long ago decided not to pay any attention to them.

"Even Dad says she's my bad omen. Something always gets loused up when she gets near me."

"Your father was joking, and this is a new home, a new page in history. Give Bertha a chance. She means well."

Bertha meant well. But she had used Jennifer's only softball jersey for a dustrag. And she had tossed Jennifer's dead insect collection, all but two hornets, into the incinerator. And once, stuffed on Bertha's cookies and sundaes, Jennifer had thrown up in the back seat going home.

"When's doomsday?"

"Tomorrow. The six A.M. express. Leave it to Bertha to wake us in the middle of the night in order to meet her at the station."

It was comforting to know that her mother wasn't exactly eager to see Bertha again.

"Hope you won't mind sleeping on the sofa, Jen,

22.

and letting Bertha sleep in your bed," her mother said.

"Not if you promise to change the sheets after she leaves," Jennifer answered.

She waited for her mother to explode. Her mother hadn't been listening . . . one of the lucky times. She kept on talking.

"Bertha wasn't sure when the workmen would finish . . . said there might be a delay in getting the fixtures. But I don't suppose she'll be here too long."

"Long enough to bring me bad luck," Jennifer thought.

Jennifer made sure she got an early start on sleep that night. She hoped she would awaken with time enough to steal away from the house before Bertha lumbered in. She dreamed that Bertha sprouted wings and crash-landed on the loft roof, scattering hay and pigeon feathers for miles and squashing Jennifer to pancake size.

The dream faded, pinched into dust and sunbeams. The clatter of breakfast dishes drifted to Jennifer's pillow from the kitchen below. Somebody tittered, then broke into chirruping laughter. Aunt Bertha.

Jennifer threw off the covers and tugged on her jeans. She searched for the Gompers School gym jersey that Bertha hated. Nowhere in sight. She settled for the embroidered blouse Bertha had given her for Christmas.

"Probably just as well to give her the thrill of her life," thought Jennifer.

She weaved her way down the stairway, wishing she were a pigeon and could flee out the window.

"Morning, Aunt Bertha," Jennifer said.

23.

She popped a piece of bread into the toaster, pulled a Twinkie from the cabinet, and poured herself a tumbler of grape soda. Bertha opened her arms for a hug and looked Jennifer over.

"Good grief, you've already outgrown that blouse—it's much too small. The child's growing like a weed. Come here and let me have a look at you."

"I feel like a piece of furniture," Jennifer said to the ceiling.

"Sit right down and your mother will have your breakfast eggs on in a jiffy," Bertha commanded.

"Jen doesn't care for eggs, remember? She wouldn't eat them if I fixed them," her mother said and retrieved the piece of toast for Jennifer. Wincing as her mother downed a glassful of carrot juice, Jennifer loaded her toast with peanut butter.

"The child's wasting away." Aunt Bertha was at it already. "That's not enough breakfast for a youngster her age."

"The age business again," thought Jennifer. "They sure are hung up on that stuff."

"It's enough. It's just not the right food," her mother said. "Don't worry, Bertha. She usually eats something other than Twinkies for breakfast."

Her father looked up from his bowl of granola. "Usually it's a big bowl of chocolate ice cream or any flavor that's available."

"I don't mind a piece of pie now and then." Jennifer figured she might as well set the record straight as long as someone was being truthful.

Her mother and her father were into health foods.

24.

Jennifer was into junk. That's what they called the stuff she ate for breakfast. It was the one meal, thank goodness, they had let her make her own. Not without a little yelling. A Twinkie was worth it.

"One can eat too many eggs, Bertha. Too much cholesterol," her mother said.

Her father shook his head, dipping into some yogurt. "See there, Bertha? This kid's not taking any chances. She eats Twinkies at the most important meal of the day."

"Well, I'll see to it that she eats more while you two are away," Bertha said as she broke off a hunk of bread with her teeth.

The peanut butter stuck in Jennifer's throat. Hadn't she told herself something rotten was in the offing? Just yesterday hadn't she predicted that Bertha would bring her bad luck?

Her father was talking. ". . . the perfect free-lance assignment. An architect's dream. Who would have suspected I'd be in the running to design it!"

He looked at Jennifer. "It'll give you a chance to be on your own."

"What will?" Jennifer asked through the peanut butter.

"A potential client called me this morning. They're building a condominium near Denver, and want me to submit plans. I'm to come up and look at the site."

Her mother smiled her get-away-from-it-all-smile. "They invited me to come along. When they offered to pick up hotel and food tabs, I couldn't resist. We'll be back before you know it, Jen."

25.

"While we're gone, you can show Aunt Bertha around," her father said, as if showing Bertha the barnyard was the greatest honor in the world.

Jennifer felt something like dynamite igniting in her stomach. She swallowed the peanut butter.

"What about back to nature? said Jennifer.

She gritted her teeth to keep the dynamite from exploding.

"Sure, that's where we are now, Jen. The city trip will only last a couple of days," her father said. "If they give me the job, I'll be able to do the work right here as we always wanted me to."

Jennifer slammed her glass down, splashing the soda all over the tablecloth. "*I* never wanted it! I'm the one who likes the city and now you're going back, leaving me here. I should be the one who's going!"

Jennifer's parents seemed embarrassed that she was making a scene. Her mother said gently, "The three of us will make the trip together next time, Jen."

She jumped up from the table and ran from the house —over the lawn, through the aspen and the patch of corn, up the ladder and into the loft, to the safe and secret room.

She hoped they never found her, ever.

4.

Imagine. If anyone loved the sweeper and the burrito man and the crowds on Sundays, or any day, it was Jennifer. She had given up Lisa and Gerard and the room on Gilpin Street because *they* had wanted to get back to nature, and now look who was going to the city.

The house on Gilpin Street was where, every Tuesday, Signe Olafson spent time with her neighborhood friends. It was the place for frying marbles into jewelry, writing poems in the dusk, dancing barefoot in finger paints, baking graham-cracker crusts, perfecting flips and cartwheels. It was the place Jennifer had loved, a part of the city she had wanted to live in forever.

Someday, she told herself, she would go back to the Tuesday place. Someday she would be a visitor. And after they had woven yarn into belts or sifted sand paintings she would sit next to Signe, where every guest sat, and tell about back-to-nature.

Her father had told her, "Someday you'll love this valley, Jen. You'll forget you ever lived in Denver."

"I won't forget," she had answered.

She wondered how long she should make them look for her. They probably figured she'd be back. They probably thought she had nowhere to go. Jennifer wished she'd brought her peanut-butter sandwich.

A murmur, soft as velvet, sifted through straw and string to Jennifer. She had forgotten the pigeons. In her fury, she had even forgotten to be afraid of the rickety ladder and the climb to the loft. Now the murmurs softened her anger. Jennifer crawled out from her secret tunnel to join the pigeons.

She knelt among them, pressing her legs and stomach and chest and cheek to the sun-warmed hay. A few pigeons bobbed over on their toothpick legs to stand

27.

face-to-face with the new neighbor. Jennifer whispered a hello.

"Would you like to be friends?" she found herself saying. "I can't fly, of course, but I've always wanted to. I have a feeling for what it's like."

She guessed that pigeons favored gentle friendships with quiet beginnings.

One, then two more birds cocked their heads to the side, as if they needed further explanation.

"I've lived most of my life in an apartment, lots higher than this place," she continued. "And now, of course, I have the secret room . . . and a bird's-eye view!"

Some of the pigeons tried to break the language barrier. They cooed a long low song of a reply. Jennifer welcomed the answer; she felt they had accepted her.

She rolled onto her side and began counting. It seemed important to know the size of her neighborhood. Jennifer stopped counting at five. Number Five sat alone at the loft doorway. Snowy white she was and silky all over. She reminded Jennifer of the Christmas card from Gerard. Jennifer had saved the card with the wonderful bird, a Number Five kind of bird, soaring alone on its cover. All white and all wings. Inside, the message had been "Peace." Number Five was peace. And Number Five was also the feeling of something lost, something special like Gilpin Street.

Number Five was smaller than the others, a pale shadow against the sky. She did not cock her head when Jennifer offered a special hello. She seemed tucked away in a kind of brooding, and Jennifer knew she should not reach out to touch her.

This bird was not like the others. She did not oil her feathers by rubbing her beak against them as Jennifer had seen the city pigeons do. She didn't bother to drink from the rain water at the loft door as two or three at a time did, sucking the water up as through a straw. She didn't even flutter her wings or break for the blue out beyond the loft and over the aspen. She was unmoving, like the porcelain bird Aunt Bertha had at home in her china cabinet.

Jennifer inched closer to the bird. Their eyes met and then Jennifer lowered hers to the nest. The base of it looked like a shallow dog dish. Beneath bits of cotton and twigs and straw, the red wool of a winter cap skimmed the dish's edge. And beneath the cuff of cap, on a curve of the bowl, was a cardboard sign with a single word crayoned in: Burma.

"Burma!" The cry came from the trees, and suddenly there was a great flapping and swishing of wings as five or six pigeons followed the echo to the trees.

The voice came again, a boy's voice, shouting the news. "Burma! I'm coming!"

Jennifer's fear pressed her to the hay. For a minute, her body was clay, as unmoving as the bird's. This very moment a boy was heading for the loft. Any minute he might discover Jennifer and her secret room. Perhaps he'd already seen her!

The bird on the Burma bowl seemed to perk up and she turned her head toward the loft opening. Jennifer, too, came to life. She dashed around the hay to the end of the barn and climbed the bales into the tunnel as fast as she was able. As she scrambled, a sneaker slipped off her left foot. Jennifer guessed that it had fallen to the loft floor or the pile of hay below and lay there now within sight of anyone. She felt the grip of fear once more, and for a moment was unable to move. Then, in a flash, she backed out of the dark corridor and hastened down the bales of hay, scooping up the shoe. As she shoved it onto her foot, the boy's feet sounded on the gravel at the barn door. Up the hay Jennifer scurried, diving into the hole in the hay. She pulled her knees up against a wall of the tunnel, tucking her feet as close to her as possible. And then, motionless in the darkness, she waited.

Jennifer's heart pounded in her ears. If the boy had not already guessed her whereabouts, he would only have to hear the pounding to find her, she was sure.

She pressed her back against the wall of hay and took three long gulps of air to calm the thumping. Her efforts failed. As the loft ladder creaked again and again beneath the boy's feet, each creak and each heartbeat came more quickly.

Jennifer's knees blocked a view of the tunnel entry. It was wiser to close her eyes to the darkness than to unwind and stretch her legs and feet to the opening and the light. Though she wanted to scream, to escape from the loft, she made not the slightest rustle in the hay. The secret room was too important to surrender.

"Burma. How ya doing, girl?" The voice of the boy

was close to Jennifer, on the other side of the tunnel wall at the loft opening.

"I'd have come sooner, but Pa wouldn't let me . . . and I have to be careful how I get here. He thinks Homer isn't going to make it back to us. We know different."

He talks to pigeons. She recognized the fact only after she had realized that her secret was safe for the moment.

That makes two of us, Jennifer thought, and smiled in the darkness.

"Homer will be coming back any day now. Then you can stop being lonely, Burma."

The boy's voice was such a sad and secret one that Jennifer was suddenly ashamed to be a wall away, listening in. It was almost as if she were the intruder, and not the boy. It was rather difficult not to eavesdrop, though, and Jennifer was interested.

"We can be alone and wait for Homer together, okay? That'll make the waiting shorter," the boy said.

Then there was quiet in the loft. Jennifer was listening and the family of pigeons was listening. There was the slightest sniffle in the silence. When the boy spoke at last, his voice was shaky, on the edge of breaking.

"Homer's just got to come back."

A high shrill whistle pierced the air. Jennifer knew the Saturday whistle of Mr. Fogarty, the eggman. He delivered fresh eggs every weekend in his pickup truck.

Every Saturday, without fail, he announced his coming with his personal whistle-between-the-teeth. And

31.

he always stopped for a cup of coffee, saying, "I can only stay for a cup's worth." Jennifer's mother and father sat him down, every Saturday, and told him about their new start in life and moving back to nature, and the eggman, every Saturday, told them nothing. Bertha would get something out of him, Jennifer figured, if anybody could.

The whistle shattered the peace of the loft again. Jennifer decided it was closer to the barn than it was to the house.

"I know you're up there, Rob. Climb down and come home with me." It was Mr. Fogarty's voice, Jennifer was certain.

There was no answer from the loft.

"Say goodbye to those birds once and for all. I warned you not to try to put anything over on me!" It was the eggman's voice again.

"The blimp squealed," the boy muttered to himself. "I bet it was the fat lady on the porch who saw me heading here."

Aunt Bertha, Jennifer thought. Bad-luck Bertha had tattled.

The boy spoke in a whisper. "I'll be back, Burma. Don't give up."

"I'll give you one more minute to come down on your own two feet!" Mr. Fogarty shouted.

Jennifer made a mental note never to eat one of his eggs again. It wouldn't be much of a sacrifice.

Rob called down to the eggman. "Pa, how about letting me take Burma home, just for tonight? She's lonely."

32.

"Get a move on," the eggman answered. The answer was neither a yes nor a no.

There was a flutter of wings and then the creak of the ladder as the boy made his way down to the floor of the barn.

Quiet returned to the old barn, broken briefly by the crunch of gravel at the entrance. Jennifer guessed that the boy had finally gone. Cautiously she moved into the secret room and eased the window open to peer out through the crack.

Mr. Fogarty stood where the cornstalks began, his arms folded across his chest. He looked annoyed as Rob walked toward him.

The boy carried a pigeon in his hands. He smoothed her feathers gently in a caress. A mumble of words, first Mr. Fogarty's, then Rob's, drifted up to Jennifer's hiding place. Though Jennifer could not make out the words, she sensed the anger in the eggman's voice. And she heard the pleading in Rob's.

Rob touched the pigeon to his cheek and then tossed her to the sky. She fluttered past Jennifer's window and down to the loft opening. Jennifer listened to the whoosh of Burma's wings as she returned to her place in the loft. She watched the man and the boy walk together through the corn and through the aspen to the yellow pickup truck. The boy's head was down. He didn't look up to say goodbye to Aunt Bertha who stood on the porch steps holding cartons of eggs. He scowled.

He crawled into the back of the pickup and hunched against a stack of cartons. Not even when the truck

33.

moved up the road did the boy lift his eyes to the loft.

Jennifer turned away, her back to the window and the light, feeling the darkness of the secret place enfolding her. Like a magician's cape, the darkness rested on Jennifer's shoulders. It swirled down over her toes.

Now Burma cooed along with the others and the sound was a lonely one. Burma cooed and the echo of the boy's words came back to Jennifer, the voice full of hurt and hoping. The eggman had chosen not to hear it, but Jennifer had listened. She looked again out the window.

She could not have moved from her place if Gerard and Lisa had appeared on the spot to call her to play. She listened to Burma and watched the yellow pickup pull a storm of dust as it moved up and around the ribbon of road. She watched it become smaller and smaller until it disappeared behind a last faraway hill.

5.

Jennifer's parents were puzzled, of course, when all she asked them to bring her from the city was a pigeon book.

"That's all you want? A book about pigeons?" her mother asked.

"How about a book about dinosaurs?" her father suggested.

"It's got to be pigeons—nothing else will do," Jennifer insisted. Why didn't grown-ups ever listen?

"I doubt if pigeon books are very popular," her mother said. "But I'll try to find one."

"I always liked dinosaurs as a kid," her father said to no one in particular.

He backed the car from the machine shed and crunched along the gravel drive. Her parents shouted directions as they backed away.

"Wear a sweater in the evenings. Eat something to please Bertha, will you?"

"And try not to give her a hard time."

"Remember, we love you."

They had turned from the yard and lurched toward the highway before Jennifer had a chance to shout, "Pigeons! Don't forget—pigeons!"

She wandered back to the kitchen where Aunt Bertha was fixing herself a chocolate sundae at the counter.

"You'll be glad you stayed with me," Aunt Bertha assured her now. "You name it, I play it. Canasta, parcheesi, checkers."

"I'm not much of a game player, Aunt Bertha," Jennifer said.

Bertha stabbed at a maraschino cherry in the jar in her hand. Her eyebrows curled into a worry frown.

"But I'm glad I stayed with you, Aunt Bertha, honest. There's lots of exploring to do."

"I'm not much of an explorer," Bertha said. "I prefer parcheesi."

Jennifer searched for a way out. "Actually, I thought I'd do the exploring and then report back to you. You're a good listener, aren't you?"

35.

"Met the Fogarty man today," said Bertha. (She hadn't been listening.) "He's a good egg if I ever met one!"

Bertha chuckled, her cheeks puffing up like dumplings. "Get it? The eggman's a good egg?"

"I get it," Jennifer said. She offered a chuckle for Bertha's sake.

"I was watering the geranium, minding my own business, when a boy sneaked out of the back of Fogarty's truck," Bertha said.

She stopped sprinkling nuts to gaze over the potted geranium on the windowsill, as if she expected to see the boy again.

"He was a quick one. Headed for the trees like a thief. But I was on the porch in a jiffy."

"You don't miss much, Aunt Bertha."

Bertha beamed, accepting the words as a compliment.

"I yelled for him to stop, but that didn't scare him. He just kept on running."

"He may not have heard you."

"Never mind. Mr. Fogarty was very upset when I reported what I'd seen."

The blimp squealed. Jennifer remembered the boy's words.

"Fogarty figured it was his youngest son. Robert's a troublemaker."

"Mr. Fogarty said that?" Jennifer asked.

"Not directly. But he said he was headstrong. He said he'd been in and out of school—a real rascal."

Bertha rummaged for a spoon in the drawers. The

36.

boy who had comforted Burma had hardly seemed a troublemaker. Jennifer did not understand.

"What was the crime in heading for the aspen?" she asked.

Bertha found the spoon and an answer for Jennifer at the same moment.

"I asked him that question in a roundabout way. He said he's forbidden the boy to come here."

"He didn't give a reason?"

Bertha frowned. "The eggman doesn't say much. Too tight-lipped for my liking."

She tasted her sundae. Jennifer grew impatient as Bertha took another spoonful. She did not want to seem too curious. She did not want Bertha to know she too had seen the troublemaker.

"I think it's dumb to forbid Robert to come here. What trouble can he cause?"

"It's not your place to question, young lady. The reason doesn't matter. Respect for elders is reason enough," Bertha said between bites. "Father knows best, you know."

Jennifer rolled her eyes to the top of her head.

"I'm lucky I got a word out of Fogarty, let alone a reason." Bertha continued. "He wouldn't even tell me much about the old man—I've forgotten his name—the one who used to live here."

It was a wild guess. Jennifer made it anyway.

"Homer? Was that his name, Aunt Bertha?"

"Doesn't ring a bell. I don't recall that Fogarty used a name. Then again, he must have."

Bertha paused, trying to remember. "Anyway, the old man took sick suddenly. A grown son appeared out of nowhere and whisked him off to Oregon without a word—that's how Fogarty put it."

Bertha shook her head sadly. "Poor old man. Never had a warning he'd be going. How would you like it if somebody came and sold your house out from under you?"

Jennifer didn't answer. She was at the door, eager to return to the loft. "I'm going exploring," she yelled.

"You let me know if you see that Fogarty boy. I promised the eggman I'd keep a lookout."

Jennifer was already running for the trees, glad not to have to answer. She ran along a path between the aspen and hurried to the loft, greeting the family of pigeons. The birds bobbed and pecked, cooed and preened, hardly noticing her.

They were Robert's birds; the loft was his. She knew it from the way he had talked to Burma; she felt it even though her parents owned the barn. The birds held secrets under their wings. They spoke a secret language. They were friends with a rascal. The birds and the boy belonged to each other.

But the hidden room behind the wall of hay belonged to Jennifer alone. It was her secret. Here, the all-alone-and-glad-to-be feeling of Sundays in the park came back to her. Here in the hay she could close her eyes and open her mind to all the questions that needed answers.

The questions were still with her at the end of the day, with guesses for answers. The guesses kept her awake in the darkened house even after Bertha had trudged to bed. By a circle of lamplight next to the sofa, she had written a list of questions to be answered by the pigeon book:

> Do pijuns have a language?
> How do you spell pijun?
> Can pijuns understand people?
> How do pijuns know which way is home?
> How far can they fly?

There was, of course, the one question no book could answer which Jennifer added, anyway, to the bottom of the list:

> Who is Homer?

She pulled a piece of tape from the roll she had brought from the kitchen and taped the pigeon questionnaire to the underside of her pillow.

She clicked off the lamp and buried her face in the pillow for a moment or two. It was always easier to listen for burglars with her face safe in the pillow. Not that the chances of meeting any away from the city were good. Just the same, the delay made the sudden blackness of the room easier to brave when she finally lifted her head to the night.

When she did, the aspen were shimmering silver under a full moon. She could see them through the window. The breeze played tag with the leaves in and out of the trees.

She was well on the way to sleep when a voice broke

the silence. The voice tried to be a whisper, but it ended as a muffled cry, not far away. It came from the aspen, perhaps, or the corn. It came too softly to stir anyone from sleeping.

Faintly, almost as if imagined, the cry formed in the darkness again.

"Burma!"

Jennifer sprang up and was at the window in a minute, her eyes fixed on the aspen. Silence. The rustle of leaves and silence. She had been sure of the voice, of the cry in the night, and waited to hear the call again. She scanned the trees for a shadow of a boy racing for the loft. She saw nothing. The longer she sat at the window, the more the voice seemed part of a dream. Wondering, fighting sleep for the sound of a boy, she finally crept back to her pillow.

Burma-Burma-Burma—the voice echoed in Jennifer's ears, and she dreamed of Rob and Homer's return.

6.

How was it, Jennifer wondered, that two days felt like two years? She listened to the wall clock and wondered if her parents would ever come back to nature. The clock ticked away forever minutes and Bertha chattered on.

"The thing about Nick Shortino is that he's always willing to do a little something extra—carry the bags up the block, fit them into my cart just right. Not like the other baggers."

42.

"I'd like to be a bagger to see what people eat," Jennifer said.

Bertha announced, "Nick likes Margaret, the cashier. But baggers can't afford to get married."

"Who'd want to get married, anyhow?" Jennifer said. She, for one, wasn't interested. No weddings for her, ever.

Bertha wasn't listening. "I'd be crushed if Nick gave up bagging to marry Margaret."

"I bet." Jennifer checked the clock—seven minutes and twenty-five seconds. Bertha had been praising Nick Shortino, supermarket bagger, for seven minutes and twenty-five seconds.

They'd spent ten minutes and fifty seconds on Lucille Majeski's wedding. That was the record—Lucille's wedding. Two minutes and ten seconds on Mrs. Coffey's soda bread. Thirty seconds on the price of noodles. Jennifer glanced at her hand under the table, the left palm where she'd penned the times for each. Nine minutes flat on Bertha's parakeet, Dicky, who'd died—a time very close, Jennifer noted, to Lucille's winning record. And five minutes on Uncle Alvin's operation.

"If I become a bagger, I'll pack the bags the best," Jennifer said. She wondered if Lucille Majeski had ever considered becoming a bagger instead of a bride.

"You'll have to be pretty special to beat Nick," Bertha said.

Eight minutes and two seconds. Nick was closing in on Dicky, the bird. Jennifer wondered, could a bagger beat both Dicky and Lucille?

"Have another macaroon," Bertha said.

So much for Nick Shortino. She jotted the time on her palm with the pen in her lap, writing under the table so Bertha wouldn't notice.

Bertha munched a macaroon, tapping a rhythm with her fingers on the lid of the parcheesi box. She had beaten Jennifer at every game of parcheesi they had played. She had trounced her four games out of four, played the endless afternoon.

Between games, Jennifer had spent time in the bathroom. Bertha had followed her everywhere ("Try one more game, Jennifer. Maybe you'll win the next one.") —everywhere but the bathroom.

Jennifer had passed the time there checking for pimples. Gerard's older brother had called them zits, which had always upset Gerard's mother who had preferred to call them blemishes. Either way, Gerard's brother had had a lot of them. (Jennifer had none.)

She had read all the labels in the medicine cabinet. Toothpaste tubes made the dullest reading, she'd decided. Jennifer had discovered patterns in the wall tiles and a razor blade in the planter on the windowsill over the tub. Staying in the bathroom wasn't as boring as being with Bertha.

Bertha didn't seem to notice that Jennifer rarely spoke.

"It's because I'm a niece and not a person," Jennifer thought.

She ate a macaroon, stuffing a few more bites of junk into her belly before her parents came home. She couldn't remember when she'd eaten so much junk. She figured it was probably her tenth or eleventh macaroon

44.

of the evening. It pleased Bertha when people ate her cookies, Jennifer reminded herself. She ate another.

Bertha thumbed through a magazine. Jennifer climbed to the attic, perching on a packing crate to watch for a sign of Robert at the loft opening, wondering for the hundredth time if she had dreamed the voice in the trees the night before. She had hurried to the loft in the morning but found no sign of a boy, no clue that he had visited. Today she had packed a shoebox for the loft—pencils and bull's-eye candies, saltines, and her music box (for Burma), a wad of Kleenex, yarn for nest making, a whistle (to use in case of danger), and a writing tablet.

She had visited the pigeons, bringing the box and a broom to sweep the loft floor. She had found a battered pan in the barn and filled it with water at a spigot in one of the stalls, carrying it up the ladder to the birds. She had cleaned the hay perches of feathers and fluff and dirt. She had climbed the bales of hay to her secret room, moving often to the tiny window. There she had watched the meadows, beyond the trees, for a sign of a boy. Robert had not appeared.

It was musty in the attic and spooky in the dark. Soon it would be too dark to see the barn from the window. She dawdled on the stairs, then headed for the sofa to check her pigeon questionnaire. It was still taped to her pillow for nightly re-reading.

Bertha was snoring in the kitchen, her head drooping on her ample chest. Jennifer watched her snore for a few minutes and then moved to the porch swing. For a while she worked on wiggling one toe at a time. She tried playing Scissors, Paper, Stone by herself, but it didn't work. She watched the stars come out.

Her mother and father finally returned, long after Jennifer had counted five hundred and twenty-three stars and grown weary of the counting. They came back with a book about dinosaurs and another entitled "Patrick Pigeon Plans a Party."

Jennifer knew without opening the book that it would answer none of her questions.

A baby book, she thought.

"Thanks for remembering," she said and gave her mother and father each a hug.

"Aunt Bertha and I were trying to remember the old man's name—the one who lived here before us," she told them.

"Olson. His last name was Olson," her father said. "I can't recall his first."

"It wasn't a common one," her mother said. "Armen or Elwood—something like that."

"How about Homer?" Jennifer asked, but her parents shook their heads.

"No, it wasn't Homer," her father said.

They gathered around the table in the kitchen. They would tell, Jennifer knew, of the two days they had spent in the city, of the fun they'd had in Denver. And Bertha would talk about winning at parcheesi and making macaroons. Jennifer felt too dejected to talk. She was tired of talking and tired of waiting. Pretending interest in the pigeon book, she left the kitchen and went to bed.

46.

Waiting for sleep, she skimmed the pages of the baby book. The first page showed a pigeon in a suit and hat, flying over rooftops. The words were large and far apart on the page:

FLYING HOME TO SUPPER ONE
NIGHT, PATRICK PIGEON GOT LOST.

Jennifer skipped a few pages, reading again.

A LONG-LOST PIGEON PAL WHISTLED
UP TO PATRICK. "COME DOWN
AND VISIT," HE SAID.

She turned the page and read on.

PIGEON PALS SOMETIMES WHISTLE
A GREETING TO FRIENDS FLYING
OVERHEAD.

"They must have taken lessons from Mr. Fogarty," Jennifer thought.

Snuggling deeper into her pillow, she grinned, feeling better somehow, and glided into sleep.

Jennifer blinked awake to find a hand resting on her head. It was her father's. He had come to waken her, as always . . . Jennifer's alarm clock.

"Morning, Jen."

Morning, yes. The couch in the living room. Sunlight on the ceiling. The crackle of paper taped to her pillow. Jennifer pushed through the fog of sleep to find her place with the day. She could hear Bertha babbling in the kitchen.

"Bertha says you were perfect company," her father

said. He paused. "Thanks for staying with her, Jen."
He gave her a hug.

Jennifer smiled, embarrassed, but pleased with herself
too.

"How about a breakfast of poached eggs and
prunes?" he asked.

"Yitch!" Jennifer doubled over.

"How about Twinkies and grape soda?"

"Now you're talking!"

In the kitchen, everybody focused on Jennifer. Con-
versation stopped between her mother and Aunt Bertha.
They looked at Jennifer and smiled, saying nothing.
Her father smiled too.

"Okay," said Jennifer suspiciously. "What's up?"

"Oh, nothing much," her father teased. "The person
I saw in Denver phoned. My chances of getting the
job look good. I'll need to make another trip to Denver
on business in two weeks."

He paused. Jennifer held her breath, wishing for the
words she wanted him to say.

"How about it?" he asked. "Will you keep me company and come along?"

"You'd better believe it!" Jennifer shouted.

She twirled in a cartwheel across the kitchen. Her
father laughed.

"How long?" she asked, gaining her balance.

He hesitated. "A Monday out at the site with me
. . ."

"And Tuesday? What about Tuesday?"

He laughed again. "Tuesday in Denver. Almost all
of it—on your own!"

"Yoweee!" Jennifer shouted.

She did four more cartwheels. The burrito man was with her on the first spin. The second twirl was for Lisa. The third was for Gerard. And the fourth brought thoughts of Gilpin Street.

Bertha's eyes followed Jennifer around the table, wide with wonderment.

"I wish I'd learned how to cartwheel," her mother said. She smiled her all-over smile and kissed Jennifer good morning.

Jennifer pulled a Twinkie from the cabinet and unwrapped it. Her mother hurried to a drawer and produced a box of birthday candles. Placing a candle in the center of Jennifer's Twinkie, her mother cleared her throat and announced:

"Ladies and Gentlemen, may I call to your attention the encouraging news that in two short weeks this child of nature will regain her city slicker status."

Her father struck a match and lit the candle. He began a few bars of the Hallelujah Chorus, the part of the Christmas music they all knew by heart. Jennifer and her mother joined in and Bertha chuckled, delighted, as they sang:

"All-leluia. All-leluia. Alleluia-alleluia.

All-lay-loo-ya!"

Pursing her lips, Bertha leaned toward the flickering candle. Jennifer dashed for the table. They blew out the flame together.

Aunt Bertha sputtered, "What a loony bunch you are . . . all loony!" Her eyes were sparkling.

Jennifer halved the Twinkie and split the halves

49.

again. Everyone, even Bertha, swallowed the chunks with much ceremony. Still humming the alleluias.

7.

"*I'm going back to Lisa and Gerard and the burrito man*," Jennifer told the birds after the morning celebration.

The birds seemed curious. Some drew closer to Jennifer. Others bobbed their heads as if eager to be a part of the excitement.

"I'll tell my friends about all of you, especially you, Burma. And maybe about Robert Fogarty. But the secret room belongs to us."

She looked out to the aspen. Had she dreamed the echo of two nights before? Had she wondered so much about Homer and Robert that she had imagined the voice in the fuzzy time between waking and sleeping?

She would ask Robert and end the wondering. She pulled the pencil and tablet from the shoebox beside her. All she had to do was to leave a mystery message, unsigned of course, in the loft. Robert was sure to find it if he returned. Perhaps he would answer it.

She wrote out the question in longhand, deciding that would look impressive:

Do you visit the loft at night?

"Awful," Jennifer mumbled, studying her penmanship.

She wrinkled the page in her fist and started again.

50.

Why is Burma sad and who is Homer?
Is he a pijun? Or is he a person?

The word Burma looked acceptable, but the pigeon-letters glared against the white of the tablet. Probably misspelled. She wadded up her second try. Into the box it went. She bent over the tablet and carefully printed the most important question:

WHO
IS
HOMER

The letters were neat and readable. Jennifer added a question mark.

?

"Who wants to know?" The words were a snarl at her shoulder.

Jennifer whirled around and found herself face to face with Robert Fogarty. He was glaring angrily at her.

Again he snapped, "Who wants to know?"

Jennifer froze. The answer wouldn't come.

"Come out! Out from wherever you are! I'll phone your father! Come out or I'll phone him!"

It was Bertha calling. Jennifer edged to the loft opening. Out of the trees waddled Bertha, holding a broom raised like a weapon. She lumbered along, puffing, spouting her warning.

Jennifer turned. She saw the fear slip not quickly enough from the boy's eyes. The eyes told her whose side she was on. She placed a finger to her lips, motioning quiet. She hurried to the ladder. Robert followed

51.

her to the edge of the opening. He watched her skim the rungs, lightning-quick, barely touching, flying to the earth below . . . out the door and smack into Bertha.

"Aunt Bertha! You've come exploring!"

Bertha was still angry. "I've come for a rascal. Come to catch that Robert Fogarty!"

Jennifer's foot drew a wing of a bird in the dust. Her thoughts raced to Robert and Burma above her, in the loft. She was their protector now.

"He was taking a shortcut, Aunt Bertha—taking some eggs to a customer up the road."

Bertha was panting. Her words came between breaths for air.

"You saw him—talked to him?"

"Only as he passed by the barn. He was in a hurry."

Bertha wiped her eyes and forehead with her big apron and sought the shade of the aspen. Jennifer followed her through the corn to the trees.

"Cookies in the oven and I go chasing that rascal. Oatmeal Supremes . . . probably burned to a crisp by now."

Jennifer resisted looking back at the loft opening. She wished Bertha would disappear. Bertha did, finally. She padded home through the trees, melting into the leaves and shade. Jennifer ran back to the barn.

At the ladder, she paused. There were no signs, no sounds, to tell her that Robert had stayed.

"He made his escape," she thought, and started her climb.

When she reached the top, there he sat, slouched

against the hay, cross-legged and cross-armed, like an Indian. The fear was gone from his eyes. His voice was no longer fierce when he spoke.

"Does she live here?"

"Just visiting," Jennifer said.

"That's her name—Bertha?"

"Bad-luck Bertha."

Robert laughed, unexpectedly; Jennifer laughed with him. Then they were quiet and rather uncomfortable. Robert rose and moved to the center of the loft. Jennifer hesitated, then followed. He stared at the birds. She knew of his sadness without asking.

Robert slammed his fist into the hay wall, startling Jennifer.

"I don't care if I *am* trespassing. I don't care if you *do* own the birds. Once they were mine."

His eyes, dark and deep-set, filled with pain again. They darted from one place to another, never looking to Jennifer. She remembered the gentle Robert Fogarty.

"The birds are yours, if you owned them first," she said.

"They were mine—a gift from a friend who used to live here. But they come with the loft. Now you own 'em," he said angrily.

"They'll always be yours," she said.

Robert was silent. He reached over and gently pulled Burma to him. She was not afraid of him.

"Not any more. Once this place was their home. Once we kept netting by the opening and feeders and nesting bowls. Now they're free to be wild."

53.

Jennifer said, "They'll stay, without the netting. It's the only home they know."

"It'd be better if they left."

Jennifer didn't understand.

"Wouldn't you miss them?" she asked.

"I'd miss 'em."

Robert paused, then spoke in anger.

"With no feeders, they'll eat the spoiled grain for food. They'll drink dirty rainwater. They'll get lice. They'll get sick. Some of 'em'll die."

Jennifer did not know what to say.

He stroked Burma and the anger fell away. He bent over the bird and seemed to forget that Jennifer was with them. She wanted to reassure him.

"City pigeons live on rainwater and scraps. I'm not sure if they get lice—but they're wild, and they always seemed healthy to me."

"I bet plenty of 'em die," he said.

Jennifer tried to remember whether she had ever come upon a dying pigeon. No, she had never seen one. Where did they go to die, she wondered? Did they burrow beneath the snow or lie in the shadows of the statues in the park . . . to leave the world gently, unnoticed? Robert broke the silence.

"You from the city—Denver?"

"Until a month ago. I lived on Gilpin Street."

"Yeah. Gilpin Street. Sure. I know where that is."

"You've been there?"

"Sure. Yeah. My ma lives near there, I think."

"I think it's the best place in the world to live."

"Maybe. One of these days my ma is coming to get me. We're gonna go live in Denver. And then probably travel around. I won't care what my pa thinks of it."

He lowered his eyes to the floor.

"Why doesn't your father want to go along?"

"They're divorced, stupe. I'm supposed to live with my pa. But one of these days, my ma's gonna kidnap me and we're gonna travel all over the place."

"Oh." Jennifer didn't know what to believe of this business of his own mother's planning to kidnap him.

"Only reason I stick around this place is to keep an eye on my friend's birds. I promised, you know. Not just anyone can take care of specially trained pigeons."

"Specially trained?"

"Sort of, anyway. Oscar banded 'em—each one has its own number. He trained 'em to race back to the loft. I helped him."

"Oh." She watched him soothe his Burma bird, calming her. "She's a nice bird, Robert."

He was silent for a moment or two.

"Only the teachers at school call me Robert. And my pa, when he's mad sometimes. My name's Rob."

"I'm Jennifer."

Rob offered his Burma-bird to Jennifer. He lifted the bird toward her.

"Here, it's your turn. She likes to be held," he said.

"I've never held a bird. I don't know how," said Jennifer.

"You'd better learn. Pigeons know you like 'em by the way you touch 'em. Cradle 'em in your hand like

55.

this, between your fingers. They like it," Rob said.

As if to agree, Burma cooed long and low into his ear. Rob held her out to Jennifer.

Jennifer's fingers fumbled for a hold. She was afraid of hurting Burma, afraid of a sudden frantic flight from her fingers to the sky. But Burma seemed to know Jennifer. She was patient and ruffled her wings only slightly as Jennifer cupped the body in her palm. Her palm felt the throbbing and the warmth of Burma. She touched a finger to Burma's head, smooth and silky. She ran it down the gentle curve of Burma's neck, smoothing Burma's wings, feeling the ridges where one feather ended and another began. Burma cooed.

"I like you, Burma," Jennifer whispered.

"She knows," Rob said.

Jennifer hugged Burma against her cheek.

"I suppose you'll be bringing a bunch of people around. Playing with the pigeons and stuff."

Jennifer said, "I told you—the birds are yours. I'm lucky just to share them with you."

Rob slammed his fist into the hay wall again. He tossed one pebble after another out the loft door.

Jennifer continued, "Besides, I don't have any friends here. I don't know anyone except you."

Rob kept tossing pebbles, saying nothing.

"Do you bring your friends here?" she asked.

He shook his head. "They'd do something mean to the birds, maybe. My buddies . . . they're okay, but they don't understand anything."

Jennifer smoothed Burma's feathers. She waited for

56.

Rob to go on. Finally, she asked timidly, "Who's Oscar? Is he an old man?"

Rob reached for Burma and gently carried her to a pocket in the hay. She peered down at Rob and Jennifer from the dark little cave in the wall.

"Yeah. He was the old guy who lived here before you came. He's gone for good."

She wondered if Rob resented her for taking his friend's place because her family wanted to move back to nature. Uncomfortable, she watched him hurling pebbles out the loft doorway.

"Bertha says you're a troublemaker," she said.

"Yep. I'm tough. My pa says I'm getting a reputation."

Jennifer knew about reputations. She had had one once for making faces. Cross-eyed lip puckers. Fat-lipped empty-eyeballed faces. People had always been asking her to do one. Even when Jennifer had grown tired of doing them, people had continued to expect them of her.

Rob stared at the clouds beyond the doorway. Jennifer recalled the mystery voice, the echo in the trees.

"Were you the voice a few nights ago, Rob?"

"Huh?"

"The voice somewhere in the trees. I thought I heard somebody calling Burma."

"You'd tell my pa if it was me, wouldn't you?"

"Of course not! It was you! You came all the way from town in the middle of the night?"

"Yeah. And it ain't the first time. I come to visit

57.

Burma and the other ones. My pa's only caught me once."

"Then you haven't given up on the pigeons."

"Who says? Sure I have. These are just visits. I can't take care of 'em like I used to."

Rob stood up and moved to the wall of hay to pat a pigeon in another hole.

"My pa don't let me come here anymore. But I sneak here sometimes like today to visit."

"I'll take care of them," Jennifer said. She'd help Rob keep his promise to Oscar!

"You? What do you know?"

"I can do it. You can teach me."

"Oh, no. Not me."

"We could save them from getting sick. They've got to have care. You said so yourself."

"I don't know," said Rob. "Lots of days I have to help my pa with chores. . . ."

"Oh, I figured that much. I can come every day. You could come only when it would be safe."

"I don't know how long I could keep coming. My ma might come any time now to take me away from here. She wrote me a letter."

Jennifer frowned. Was this just an excuse to give up?

"Look, you made a promise to Oscar. These birds need you. And I'll help you. That's all."

Rob turned her way, his face hopeful. Jennifer guessed that she was beginning to convince him.

"Where's the netting, Rob? We'll start right now."

"Wait a minute. The netting's too heavy to put up

ourselves. We'd have to be satisfied with feeders and stuff at first."

"Okay. Where are they?"

"I hid 'em in a shack nearby." Rob looked sheepishly at Jennifer. "Oscar *did* give me the stuff along with the birds . . . and I didn't want the new owners to throw any of it out."

Jennifer giggled. "Can you bring the stuff here if I promise not to throw any of it out?"

"Sure I can. Next time I slip out here, I'll bring all of the equipment up to the loft."

Jennifer jumped to her feet and spun around. She felt sky-high. She started a chant.

"We can do it. We can do it. We can save the birds."

Rob laughed at her, but he looked happy too.

"There are male birds, penned up at my cousins' ranch. Oscar's son took 'em there before he left, to keep these birds from having babies."

"How will we get them back?"

"Leave it to me."

They heard it together, the rumble of the pickup. It chugged and coughed over the gravel road, spitting stones and dust from beneath its wheels.

"I'll tell you the birds' names next time." He hurried to the ladder.

"When?" Jennifer asked.

Rob shrugged. He climbed down the ladder, then shouted his promise up to Jennifer from the floor below.

"I'll be back soon! And I'll get the other birds back here too. That's a promise!"

59.

He ran from the barn. Jennifer darted to the loft opening. The question came to her and she shouted it to Rob.

"Who is Homer?"

Her words were lost somewhere between the barn and the flying red of his jacket. She watched him skim a nearby field as he headed for the roadside. A blur of red disappeared beneath the bridge that crossed the creek.

The truck belched its way around the curve of road, the eggman at the wheel. It slowed at the bridge, and Rob sprang from his hiding place into the back of the truck before it picked up speed.

The secret room was a good place in which to wonder. Jennifer sought it out now.

"Come back soon," she said to the patch of sky beyond her window, already eager for Rob's return.

8.

"Buffalo Bill bedded down in Del Norte over a hundred years ago," she wrote on the post card to Gerard. Chuckling, she added, "I wonder where his buffalo slept?"

Jennifer sat on the curbing of Grand Street in Del Norte. As she wrote she watched grandmother wedgies, cowboy boots, and mountain shoes with thick soles and heavy laces pass her by on what had once upon a time been the Navaho Trail. Her parents would have preferred to stay home rather than travel to the Del Norte

Birthday Celebration—just a gimmick to drum up tourists, they had guessed—but she and Bertha had wanted to go. Bertha had been ready before breakfast, in her pink petal hat with her handbag in her lap.

Men in ten-gallon hats, chunky ladies, and kids in groups and in pairs went in and out of the stores, up and down the sidewalks. Jennifer was the stranger, alone on the curb. She pretended to be busy with her dime-store buys. She checked the water pistol, a steal for twenty cents, and the cricket cage, the band of button candy, and the rhinestone yo-yo.

Her thoughts were of Robert Fogarty. He had forgotten—he must have forgotten—his promise to bring back the birds. She was thinking of her visits—twice a day for a week, almost two, only to find, every time, an empty loft. She had become angry with hoping and hurrying to the barn and finding nothing changed, no one there. She had come to hate him for not coming.

She would quit counting on a troublemaker. Instead she'd think of the trip to Denver only two days away.

She mailed the card. She filled the pistol at the Del Norte Mineral Water Well. (Fancy name for a drinking fountain, Jennifer thought.)

She looked up and down Grand Street and, against her will, made a wish that Rob would appear. Aunt Bertha was waving for Jennifer to join her and another woman. As Jennifer shuffled toward Bertha, her parents strolled out of the pottery shop and joined them.

"Meet Mrs. Priebe," said Aunt Bertha. "She owns a grocery store in town. I've invited her to lunch with us."

61.

Mrs. Priebe smelled of salami and cheese. Jennifer was not interested in her or in lunch, but she tagged along.

Lunchtime, and boys hawked canteloupes and watermelons. Men in white aprons scooped up barbecues on the lawn of the First Baptist Church. Families ate sack lunches on the tailgates of their pickup trucks. Boys and girls slurped sno-cones at a corner stand. Bertha led the way to the Ponderosa Café, where she insisted on a booth.

"Before my legs give out," she said.

They found one, with a view of the street. Over the edge of her menu, past the plate glass, Jennifer watched a motorcycle weave up Grand.

Shiny with chrome, it flashed in the sunlight. The driver, tall and gangly, wore overalls, and a cap over haystack hair. The cycle roared past Jennifer at the window. On the back fender, in an oversized helmet and clinging to the overalls, was Robert Fogarty.

Jennifer stopped a cry halfway to her throat. She felt the squeeze of Mrs. Priebe on one side of her, Aunt Bertha on the other. There was the plate glass between her and the reason for calling out.

He was gone. The waitress stood ready to take an order. Jennifer ordered last—cheese burritos with a side order of fries and catsup—and, later, listlessly ate, forgetting to enjoy her usually favorite lunch. The lunch hour stretched to an hour and a half. The air conditioning made Jennifer's skin prickly with goose bumps.

"25¢ SPECIAL: CARTOONS AT THE LIBRARY" read the sign in the hardware store window across the street.

62.

"Cartoons for me," Jennifer announced.

She crawled over the salami-and-cheese lady and out of the booth. Her father glanced at his watch.

"Be back at the car in an hour, Jen."

She headed east along Grand Street toward the library. She found the farm boy instead, sitting on his cycle at the corner. Looking embarrassed, he thrust a note into her hands:

DEL NORTE BIRTHDAY SPECIAL: 25¢ CYCLE RIDE

Jennifer stepped to the curb. She eyed the cycle. It was enormous. Once she had taken a putt-and-sputter ride around the block on Gerard's brother's motorbike. Her parents had not minded then. She fished for a quarter. Around the block, perhaps, and she'd be back at the corner. No harm in a trial run around the block, she thought.

Jennifer lifted the helmet over her head. She felt drawn to the cycle. It gleamed at the curb, waiting to roar. With a backward glance toward the café, just out of range, Jennifer handed the boy her quarter. Blushing, he tucked it into his pocket. As Jennifer fastened the helmet and climbed aboard, he revved the motor.

The vision of Rob riding the cycle returned. She dug her fingers into the cloth of the overalls.

"Hold on tight now. Keep your feet up," were his only words.

The helmet wobbled on her head. The roar of the cycle whirred in her ears. They glided from the curb and pushed away toward a towering hill looming above the housetops.

63.

As they picked up speed, the wind swept against Jennifer's face. Passersby waved to the driver. He said nothing. Nor did Jennifer above the roar of the engine.

He headed west along sleepy side streets, away from the cluster of schools now in sight. She was glad they would not be nearing the buildings where everybody, through twelfth grade, went to school. She liked to pretend that school here would never start. Summer could last forever as far as Jennifer was concerned.

Her hair streamed behind her. The wind touched her shoulders. Peeking over the boy's shoulder, she saw the road stretching out before her. They passed the Trading Post selling shiny cycles out front, and Grand Street became the highway, pushing west.

They zoomed past cattle and barbed wire, and horses lifted their heads as they passed. The fields of wild-flowers became clouds of misty lavender and yellow. The leaves and branches of a tree here and there rushed away behind them. Del Norte was out of reach. This was no round-the-block-run.

A fear pushed itself into Jennifer's thoughts, a city fear. "Kidnapped?" she wondered, but she remembered the waving passersby and Rob on the fender. If there were any suspicious strangers in town, she figured, they were herself and her family. She was not afraid.

She took in great gulps of air. It rushed up her nostrils into her mouth. She smelled the blend of cattle and hay and manure and liked it. She smiled into the wind and sky. The road belonged to the cycle, and the miles of fields belonged to it too.

Jennifer was suddenly glad to have a part of the land

for her own, glad for her share of pasture and for the stream that rippled under the bridge near the barn. She wanted to reach out for a pocketful of wildflowers.

". . . or a fistful of sun," she thought, reminded of her father.

The white of the house and the bark of the aspen loomed ahead. The boy turned his cycle toward the familar buildings, Jennifer's home. Jennifer was thinking of how she would tell Lisa and Gerard of the cycle ride, when the cycle sputtered to a stop.

The boy turned and spoke. "Head for the loft. I'll be back."

Jennifer searched his face. Was this a trick?

"My parents . . . I have to be back in town soon," she stuttered.

"I'll be back," he said again, motioning toward the barn.

It stood across the meadow, beyond the aspen. And in the loft opening was a patch of bright color—a boy in a red jacket, waving wildly.

"Is it Rob?" she asked, knowing already.

The driver nodded. "I'll be back to fetch you soon. Don't worry."

He drove away. Jennifer scrambled under the barbed wire and headed across the meadow. She stumbled on stubble, then a furrow. Prickly weeds scratched at her knees and ankles. It didn't matter.

Jennifer was laughing and the voice inside her was singing, "My friend—my friend!"

She paused at the edge of the field, panting for breath as Bertha had done.

65.

"Hurry, Jennifer!"

Rob's voice came muffled across the distance between them. Jennifer raised her shoulders, stretching for breath to carry her to the loft. Her eyes were on the earth flying away beneath her feet. She watched her sneakers leap over stones and roots, as if to prove to herself that she was covering ground. She was almost there, bypassing the trees, cutting through the corn. A last spurt of energy brought her to the barn door.

Looking down through the hole in the loft floor, Rob crouched at the ladder. The corners of his smile reached almost to the tips of his ears.

She hurried past the top rung to the center of the loft, falling against the hay, the sweet warm scent of it all around her. The birds cooed a welcome. She slid on her back to the floor, arms outstretched, head back, catching her breath. She gazed up into the rafters, and then out to the upside-down-world beyond the loft door.

"They'll be here any minute. Keep your eyes on the sky."

Jennifer sat up, alarmed.

"Who's coming?"

"The birds, Jennifer. Have you forgotten already?"

Forgotten? How could she have forgotten his promise?

"They're coming home today?"

Rob grinned again, looking to the sky and trees.

"Any minute. My cousin Ernie's gone to free 'em. I told him you wanted 'em back . . . seeing as they came with the loft."

68.

Rob sat down, his eyes on the blue and the clouds, watching for the birds. "Ernie's the guy who drove you out here. That wasn't easy, you know, getting Ernie to give you a ride. He's shy of folks, especially girls."

"He doesn't talk much."

"Good thing," said Rob. "I don't want folks knowing I'm out here. Or that Ernie went and freed the birds. His family's been keeping the males at their place."

"Won't Ernie get into trouble? Won't he tell on you?"

"Naw. His folks ain't interested in birds. They won't even notice they're gone, I expect. Besides, Ernie thinks you asked for the birds."

"Well I did, in a way."

"Ernie did it as a favor, too. He don't say much, but I guess he kind of sees I need to be out here, waiting and having the birds, all of 'em, here."

Jennifer thought of the waiting—of Rob and Burma waiting together to make the time shorter and easier.

"Who is Homer?" she asked, softly, afraid that he would not tell her.

Rob said nothing for what seemed a very long time. He broke a straw in half, then again. His eyes followed the zigzags of a gnat in the air.

Finally, Jennifer made her guess. "He was a bird, a pigeon, wasn't he?"

"My favorite bird, a racing homer. The best flier of all the homers."

"And he flew away?"

69.

"He wouldn't have left Burma for anything! She was his mate and most pigeons mate for life." He sounded angry as if he thought Jennifer was stupid to think Homer had flown off. He picked up Burma and smoothed her feathers. He closed his eyes. "I sent him to Oscar in Oregon," he said into her wings.

"Wow! Oregon? All the way to Oregon?" Jennifer couldn't hide her surprise. "How will he make it back from Oregon?"

"What do you know, stupe? Huh?! Oscar and me always said Homer could make it if we sent him. We knew he was smart enough and strong enough to fly thousands of miles to make it home. He'll be back. What do you know about racing homers? He'll be back."

Rob kicked at the wall of hay.

"My pa tries to make me forget Homer by keepin' me away from here. 'It don't help to mope around there,' he keeps tellin' me. 'Stay away.' But I ain't givin' up."

Jennifer wondered whether Oscar had been daring enough to let Homer fly home. Oregon was far away —over a thousand miles, Jennifer knew. A long flight for even the best of the racing homers.

"I put Homer in the van. I sneaked him into the back with a note when the movers weren't looking."

"Did the note ask Oscar to send Homer back?"

A few birds cocked their heads, as if they too waited for an answer.

"Naw. Oscar would know to send him back . . . to prove Homer could do it like we always said. This was

70.

a chance to prove that Homer could make it home."

Burma fluttered out of his hands to a hole in the hay.

"I just said thanks. He was my friend. I had to say goodbye."

In Jennifer's mind, the moving van climbed the mountains, winding around hairpin curves. It pierced tunnels. It zoomed over highways through green forests. On it rolled to Oregon, with Homer and the love message tucked inside.

Jennifer wondered if anyone had found Homer in the van and if anyone had known enough to give the pigeon to the old man. She wondered if Rob wondered too. There were a lot of ifs. There were a lot of reasons Homer might not make it home. But it was best not to think of those reasons now. It was better to think of the reasons he had to make it home, to Rob and to Burma, and to Jennifer too.

Jennifer looked away. It was then, with her gaze on the blue beyond the loft, that she saw the first dot against the sky. Then another. Then one, two, three more.

"They're coming!" she cried.

Rob sprang to his feet, poised, arching as if readying himself to fly. Jennifer jumped to his side. They shouted their welcomes. Burma fluttered from the hay, leading the other birds into the sky. The welcoming committee.

The dots of gray became specks, and then the wings were clear against the sky.

"How did they know to come back here, after Ernie freed them?" Jennifer asked excitedly.

71.

"They're racing homers, trained to come home to their loft. Oscar trained them . . . and I helped."

One by one, the pigeons fluttered to the loft opening. The chatter of the birds surprised Jennifer. Grunts, coos, and high-pitched squeaks filled the room with pigeon greetings.

"They're all together again," Jennifer said, watching the reunion in wonder. "You didn't forget your promise."

Rob frowned, looking out the doorway. "I didn't know whether I should keep it. I stayed away not knowing."

"Afraid you'd get in trouble?"

Whirling on Jennifer, startling the birds, he yelled, "I'm not afraid of anything! I'm not afraid of you or anybody!" He sneered at Jennifer. "I waited to see if you'd turn me in. I made certain you hadn't gone and squealed."

Now Jennifer was angry. "I don't rat! I told you I wouldn't tell!"

He yelled back. "You could have!"

She yelled louder. "I *could* have!"

Rob looked into her face, confused, then he turned away, retrieving Burma. His words were a mumble. "But you didn't."

Jennifer's voice quieted too. "I wouldn't. Ever."

He handed Burma to Jennifer. They sat, bird-watching, letting the minutes pass without words, only pigeon talk.

Jennifer grinned, remembering. "For a second, I thought Ernie was a kidnapper."

Rob let out a squeal, as if he'd been tickled. "Ol' Ernie? He wouldn't hurt a fly!"

"Did you order him to take me here?"

"Heck no, Jennifer. He did it as a special favor."

Rob told her how he had spied her writing the post card and decided on the spot to do the flyer.

"Ernie understands. He's a pal of my older brothers, but he don't pick on me the way they do. He knows I won't give up. He knows why I slip out here, even when my pa says not to."

"You're waiting for Homer," she said.

Rob nodded. He and Jennifer heard the hum of the cycle, returning.

"Gotta scoot. See ya in a day or two," Rob said and disappeared through the hole and down the ladder. He was gone before she could tell him about leaving for the city. She left the birds and walked through the meadow. There was no sign of Rob anywhere.

Ernie was waiting. He returned her quarter, blushing again, and they headed for town.

Jennifer loved the ride back to Del Norte.

"Just like in a book," she thought, savoring the adventure of the ride to the barn and the secret return of the birds while the eggman and Bertha and her mother and father were in town.

She and Ernie returned to town not a minute too soon. Ernie zoomed to a side street, in view of the car. Bertha's pink petal hat peeked over the ledge of the back seat. Her legs had given out.

Her parents trudged around the corner, carting boxes of geraniums and a big pottery vase, looking pleased that

73.

they had spent their money. They busied themselves with loading the trunk. No one noticed Jennifer slipping from the cycle.

"Not that it would matter," Jennifer thought, and was glad, anyway, that no one had seen her.

Her father hummed as he drove home. "Ready to go to a real town on Monday, Jen?" he asked.

"Uh-huh," Jennifer said, wishing she had told Rob about her plans.

"Ready to visit all your old haunts?" her mother asked.

"Uh-huh." Jennifer said, wishing she were there already.

9.

*The city bus to Gilpin Street edged to the curb to de-*posit passengers. Jennifer peered from the windows, looking for a familiar face. She had posted herself at her favorite lookout, the rear center seat that faced the aisle, and had checked out every embarking traveler.

A nun with faraway eyes and a pale smile hurried up the sidewalk to the bus, a rabble of campers behind her. Two campers climbed the steps. They found the remaining empty seats.

The other campers lagged behind on the curbing, clustered around a man offering free balloons with "Grand Opening: Pasta Palace" printed on each one.

"Red. Gimme the red one."

"A green one, please."

"Got a polka-dot one, mister?"

The nun leaned out of the bus doorway, urging the campers to hurry. "We'll be late for song hour, children. The bus driver is waiting." Still smiling, she turned to the bus driver. He scowled. Back to the door she turned, her voice now the crack of a whip.

"Stop dawdling. Get on this bus, pronto."

One by one, the campers squeezed their balloons through the doorway and into the face of the bus driver. Filled with helium, the balloons bounced along the ceiling, over the heads of the passengers who grunted and mumbled and ducked from the lowest ones.

Jennifer watched as the aisle flooded with white camper shirts. The black-and-white nun was a ship above the waves of white and the sky was red and orange and green and yellow polka dots.

Jennifer saw her then—the camper playing paddle ball on another kid's head, then against the ceiling. It was Lisa.

"Lisa! Lisa Romano! Leeesah!"

The man next to Jennifer squinched down into a little knot as she screamed.

"Lee-sah!"

Lisa jumped up and down to peek over the heads, between the bouncing balloons. Sighting her friend, she squealed a hello.

"Jennifer! Yowee!"

They were many heads away from touching. Lisa squirmed onto a seat and balanced over the bald head of a passenger.

"What are you doing here?"

75.

Jennifer shouted back. "I'm on my way to Gilpin Street to surprise everybody. Today's my only time to see you!"

Lisa pointed to her t-shirt. Jennifer read the lettering across the chest: Holy Angels Day Camp.

"I'm a Holy Angel. Would ya believe it?" Lisa yelled.

"What about Gilpin street, our Tuesday place?"

"Gerard's there and everyone else. I gotta go to church day camp for two weeks. My mother says I need some moral development."

"How do you get that?"

Lisa giggled. "You make cruddy wallets and go to catechism."

The nun with the faraway eyes squinted them into two little slits, focusing on Lisa. Lisa didn't notice.

Jennifer yelled in order to be heard. "Why are you on a city bus?"

"We went to the park. The church bus is getting fixed. I'll get off at Gilpin with ya. They'll never miss me."

Jennifer knew better. While Lisa studied the shine on the bald man's head, the nun studied Lisa and edged up behind her.

Jennifer struggled toward her friend, hoping to warn her. Under an arm, over a shoe, around a shoulder, into an elbow, past the balloons . . .

"Gilpin Street," mumbled the bus driver.

There was no time to help her. Lisa was on her own.

Jennifer squeezed through the t-shirts, kicked, elbowed, free at last. She watched from the curb as Lisa moved toward the middle door. Lisa reached the step, almost free, when the nun pounced. In one swoop she pulled her up by the t-shirt and back into the fold. Lisa yelped a goodbye. Jennifer waved. The Holy Angels glided away from the bus stop, Lisa among them.

Jennifer crossed the street, heading for the room on Gilpin Street. The Tuesday people would be there to greet her, all her friends on the block and Signe Olafson too.

They would ask her many questions: Do you have a mountain in your back yard? Is there a stream for fishing? What things are there to climb? (The last from Gerard.)

Perhaps there would be a sand painting to do and, on the roundabout way home, a burrito for each from the burrito man, if they had enough change among them.

Jennifer skipped to the house and touched the sign that hung over the buzzer—"Arts and Things Crafty"—then the buzzer.

Brinng. Brinngg.

Sven, the Swede who swept the sand from the floor and the dust from the sills, answered the bell.

"Ya? Iss Yennifer!" he said. "Has Yennifer come back to us?"

Jennifer smiled. "Just to visit."

"Nobody here but me and de cat." Sven looked troubled. "Dey vent to de museum, yust about tirty minutes ago."

"Which museum, Sven?"

Sven shook his head sadly. "I forget to ask vich. Some museum. Vere do ya tink dey headed?"

Jennifer could not guess. "I don't know."

She stood at the door, wanting to move inside. More than anything, she yearned to enter and climb the stairs to the cluttered room of the Tuesday people. She wanted to sit again amidst the jumble of easels and tables and pillows, pretending her friends were with her. She only had to close her eyes and imagine everything was the same as always. She could pretend. But she was embarrassed to ask, afraid Sven might think her silly.

"Tell Gerard I was here, please."

"Ya. Yerard vill be sorry he missed his friend Yenny."

Jennifer walked to the bus stop.

There was nowhere to go. She was closer to her friends than she had been in weeks, yet just as far away. They were gone until long after lunch, and Jennifer would be on her way home by then.

She decided on a burrito. A burrito would help. She raced for the corner where the old man peddled them.

He was not there. The cart stood where it always had, but no one cried, "Boooreeetohss!" A skinny boy leaned against the cart, reading a comic book.

"Is the old man gone?"

The boy did not look up when he answered her. "Yeah. Split to California. Wanna burrito?"

"I was counting on seeing him. And he's gone."

The boy looked up. "So what? The burritos taste the same."

"Not to me," she said.

She took the bus to the park. She found a flock of pigeons near the fountains. They reminded her of the family in the loft. Farther along the pathway there was her favorite statue, just as she had left it.

A cowboy still struggled atop a bucking horse. The bronco reared and strained to throw the rider. The rider gripped the saddle, too proud to give in. They would always be there, neither giving in. Statues didn't go to day camp or move to California.

A young man sat curled beneath the bronco's hoofs. He wore a purple satin shirt, soft and shiny, and he had a ring in one ear. One hand held a harmonica to his lips. He played it slowly and sleepily. His other hand dipped into a brown bag beside him; he beckoned to the birds and teased them with crusts that he pulled from the bag. They came and bobbed for bread. He offered some crusts to Jennifer.

"Thanks," she said, admiring the man's kinky-crinkly hair that framed his face like a halo. She tossed the crusts and the pigeons scurried to the feast.

"The bench folk fatten the birds on crackerjack and oreos," he said. "Gonna sweet-tooth them pigeons to death."

"Bread's better," Jennifer agreed.

He seemed like the kind of person in whom she could confide. "I'm looking for a lost pigeon. His name is Homer."

She felt a bit silly having given a name, but the man didn't seem surprised.

"Homer? Nobody I know jumps to that name. No Homer here."

No Homer. The words made Jennifer feel empty. "He's a special bird. A boy I knew sent him to Oregon and he hasn't come home. He's long overdue."

"That bird's banded if he's a homer. Haven't seen a band on a bird yet. Not in this park."

Jennifer blurted the question she had kept from Rob, but wondered to herself. "Do you think he was . . . injured maybe or . . . killed somehow . . . coming home?"

The young man scratched his fuzzy head and shot a glance at Jennifer. "More likely, he took a detour. That's it. The dude took a detour."

Patrick Pigeon came to mind. Patrick had interrupted his travels to greet a friend.

"No," Jennifer thought. "That's baby stuff. Make-believe."

The harmonica man continued. "They're sociable, pigeons are. Some poor devil winging home on the wind hears a brother whistle a welcome—why, he's down in a flash. Ten to one, Homer's found some new kinfolk."

The last thing Jennifer wanted to hear was a ten-to-one bet that Homer wouldn't be back. It had been bad enough wondering whether he had been injured or killed. It was almost worse to think that he had simply not bothered to come home.

"He'd never forget Burma," she said.

The harmonica man nodded toward a couple of old

people on a bench and shook his head: they were breaking up a Nestle's Crunch for the birds.

Beyond the bench across the street was the library. A book might hold the answer . . . tell what Homer might be up to. Perhaps a book would prove the harmonica man wrong. She darted for the library, waving a hasty goodbye. Down the steps, through the doors to the children's room, she marched to the card catalog. "P for pigeon," she mumbled, thumbing through the cards.

"How about *Heroic Pigeons* or a Boy Scout book on pigeon raising?"

A very tall woman leaned over Jennifer's shoulder, looking at the cards. A tag pinned to her white shirt said "Minnie Simmons." Minnie Simmons belonged to the library. She stood, waiting for an answer.

"Uh, yes please. Anything on pigeons."

Jennifer ran after Minnie Simmons, whose stork legs took giant strides across the room, up and down the rows of shelves. She piled the books into Jennifer's arms. Then she was off to help someone else fingering the cards—G for Giants, S for Snakes, X for Xylophone.

There was so much to read about pigeons. So many people had discovered them before Jennifer had! She flipped the pages, reading snatches of words in one book, then another.

"Famous Pigeons" was the title of a chapter in one of the bigger books. Midway down the page Jennifer read, "Frisco Lady, a racing homer, flew from San Francisco to New York."

Jennifer felt her eyes growing wide as she stared at the page. San Francisco to New York? Why, that was over three thousand miles!

She read on about brave birds—Cher Ami and G.I. Joe and Leyden—birds who, carrying messages, had saved troops and towns.

"Burma Queen," she read, "a racing homer, flew three hundred and twenty miles over some of Burma's highest mountains in nine hours. The bird carried information which helped bring a battle to a close."

"Burma!" Jennifer cried aloud.

Minnie Simmons advanced to the table, not minding the shouting out.

"That's a place in India," she said, smiling.

"Burma, *this* Burma's a bird, the one in the book and another one. A bird in our loft. Our bird's name is Burma!"

Minnie Simmons read to herself the part about Burma Queen, her lips moving around the smile as she read.

"Your Burma is a namesake," she said. "Named after the famous Burma Queen. That's quite an honor for a bird. Is she a good flier?"

"Burma doesn't fly much," Jennifer told her. "She just waits for Homer to come back to her."

Minnie Simmons looked puzzled.

"Homer's the flier—the best of the lot," she said.

"Oh. And how long has Homer belonged to you?"

Jennifer stared blankly at the librarian. How long? Why, she had never even seen Homer; she didn't even know what Homer looked like. Homer had never belonged to her.

84.

"Homer's coming back from Oregon, any day now," she mumbled, ignoring the question.

Something else disturbed Jennifer—something in the words she had read: "three hundred and twenty miles in nine hours."

She scanned the pages, checking times and distances. The famous birds had flown many miles in a matter of days. And Homer had been gone for weeks.

"Homer isn't coming back." She tried to push the thought away.

The librarian had moved on to other people. The long table, the towering rows of books, made Jennifer feel suddenly very lonely. She felt like a stranger, as if she didn't belong.

She left the table of books, fighting the miles on her mind—miles that kept friends from each other.

"You got a loft?" It was the harmonica man, calling from his place on the statue as she passed.

Jennifer halted. "Not in the city. I don't live here anymore."

A lump came to her throat. The words had surprised her. She wondered how it had happened, the moving away and slipping from belonging to Gerard and Lisa and the Denver people. They were gone to camp or the museum or California, without her. Jennifer wanted to touch them and know she belonged. But they were anywhere but here. Without them, nothing was the same.

"I came back to see my friends," Jennifer said. "They aren't around. Even the burrito man is gone."

The man played a few notes, slow and sad, on his harmonica.

He sighed. "Things are always changing. Cling to today, sister. You can't go back."

Jennifer watched as he put his harmonica in a shirt pocket. He crumpled the bag and arched it, aiming for a distant wastecan. It missed.

"Today I go back to nature," Jennifer said. There's somebody there who might be my friend."

He grinned, ambling toward the bag in the grass. "Now that's good. Nothing like a brother—" he glanced at Jennifer, "a *friend*—to light up the day."

He waved to her. She smiled and waved back. She tried thinking, as he had told her to do, of today. She said a silent goodbye to Gilpin Street. She wished the burrito man well at his new corner in California. She thought about returning to the loft. Wouldn't Rob be proud when he learned that Burma was a namesake? Perhaps he already knew. Was he waiting in the loft, hoping for her return? Was he willing to be her friend?

She counted the hours away from going home. Back to Burma and Rob and the bluer sky. Back to nature in Del Norte where she almost belonged. Where she would belong, someday, if she made a friend.

In the car with her father, Jennifer counted many miles and hours before they sighted the white house and the barn and the aspen. It took only a few moments, however, to sense that something was unusual about this homecoming. The sight on the front porch was a strange one. It made Jennifer sit up and press her face against the windshield. Her father noticed, too, and forgot to tell Jennifer to sit back.

Her mother stood on the steps, waving her greeting. Behind her sat Bertha, looking very stern and forgetting to wave a hello. In one hand was the broom. Sharing the porch swing, squinched up next to Bertha and looking very nervous, sat none other than Robert Fogarty.

10.

Jennifer's mother smiled, as if nothing could be more natural than Bertha's sharing a swing with a rascal.

Why were they sitting together anyway? Jennifer thought of perfectly ridiculous reasons.

"Rob set the barn on fire by mistake and Bertha is going to take him to jail." (The barn, of course, was still standing.)

She thought of possible reasons, like: "Rob called Aunt Bertha a blimp to her face and Aunt Bertha called his father to come and get him."

The looks on their faces told her they had not taken a liking to each other while she had been gone. It wasn't friendship that had brought them together on the swing.

"Robert has been waiting for you, Jen," her mother said.

"Hurumph," said Bertha. "That's what he'd have us believe."

"He was waiting all afternoon by the roadside," her mother added.

"Hiding in the ditch," corrected Bertha.

Jennifer's mother continued, "We invited him to wait with us on the porch."

Rob eyed the broom.

"Bertha chased him, thinking he might be heading for the barn, against his father's wishes. But we straightened out the misunderstanding."

"I know a rascal when I see one," Bertha muttered.

Jennifer's mother smiled nervously. "Today Bertha tried some of my natural foods in one of her cooky recipes. Why don't we all have some."

"How about it, Rob?" her father said. "Will you join us?"

"I've got to be going," Rob said.

"You can't go! Not yet!" Jennifer pleaded. "Stay for cookies, Rob, please!"

He gave in, shrugging his shoulders. "Okay."

Bertha turned to Jennifer, obviously astonished, as if she only now could imagine that Jennifer did, indeed, know a rascal—that she might, good heavens, even be friends with one. Her eyes, full of surprise, moved from Jennifer to Rob and back to Jennifer.

They headed for the kitchen, Rob and Jennifer lagging behind the others.

"When you didn't come to the loft, I thought you were sick or something," he whispered.

"I went to Denver. I forgot to tell you I was going," Jennifer whispered back.

"I found out—after Bertha spooked me with the broom!"

Jennifer giggled. The grownups prepared the table

and food. Rob wrote on a paper napkin with the pencil from his shirt pocket:

I MOVED STUFF TO LOFT. OSCAR WOULD BE GLAD.

Jennifer wrote back:

BURMA IS A NAMESAKE. A BOOK SAYS SO.

Rob took the pencil. He wrote:

SOME BIRDS MAKING NESTS ALREADY.

"Let's hear about your trip to the city," her mother said, sitting down at the table.

Absentmindedly Jennifer offered, "I found out more about pigeons."

"Now that I think of it, someone told me Olson was a fancier—he raised pigeons," her father said. "There are some in the barn, Jen. I've seen them."

"Have you or Rob seen any?" her mother asked.

Jennifer looked at Rob gulping his milk, his eyes wide with fear above the rim of the glass. She did not care to imagine what his father would do if he found out about Rob's forbidden visits.

"I've seen some," Jennifer mumbled. "Pass the cookies, please."

"Great cookies," Rob said quickly.

Bertha beamed. "Oatmeal Supremes—with honey and wheat germ in them."

Rob chewed and smiled, looking uneasy.

"Burned the last batch to a crisp, chasing a—" Aunt Bertha stopped. Her face reddened. "Have another," she said abruptly, passing the plate.

Rob smiled and Jennifer smiled. They kicked each other under the table and tried not to laugh. Jennifer warded off more pigeon questions.

89.

"Lisa Romano is a Holy Angel for two weeks. Gerard was at a museum. The burrito man split to California. And I talked to a man who plays a harmonica in the park."

"Oh my!" cried Bertha. "Didn't your parents ever teach you not to speak to strangers?"

"He was nice, Aunt Bertha."

"Nice! What is nice?" Aunt Bertha exclaimed. "He could have kidnapped you."

Jennifer's parents looked concerned. She felt a lecture coming.

"Someday Rob's mother's coming back to kidnap him," she said, trying to change the subject.

Rob sat up straight in his chair. His face drained white and his eyes grew big. He stared, horrified, at Jennifer. Jennifer guessed her blunder and stared, helpless and sorry, back at him.

"I made that up," Rob mumbled. "It was a joke— she never really said that."

The grownups glanced nervously from Rob to Jennifer and then at each other.

Rob gave a little laugh that came out a squeak. "Kidnap me—ha! My ma don't want me. It was only a joke."

Her father cleared his throat and tapped a finger on the tabletop. Her mother slid her chair back and moved to pour herself more tea at the stove.

"Well, it sounds as if you had a busy time in the city, Jen."

Only Bertha still studied Rob. Her eyes were soft as she watched the boy staring down at his hands. She looked, to Jennifer, as if any minute she would take Rob and hug him close against her apron.

"Before you and Jen returned, I called Mr. Fogarty," her mother told her father. "I told him we'd invited Rob to wait with us and that I hoped he wouldn't be angry that Rob was here. He said it was all right this time."

Bertha added, "She said you'd drive Rob home."

"A good idea," her father said. "That means Rob can stay longer. Right, Rob?"

He looked up. "I guess so."

Bertha gathered up the plates and napkins, Rob's among them. She read the words scrawled on his napkin and glanced at Rob. Crumpling up the napkins, she moved from the table.

"Kind of queer—no disrespect intended, of course— but kind of queer that Mr. Fogarty has such a grudge against that loft. Lord knows, somebody's got to keep an eye out for the birds in the barn."

Rob's eyes followed Bertha as she moved from the table to the sink, then back again.

"I've a notion to talk some sense into that man. Goodness knows, nobody here minds if this fancier— pigeon fancier—" she said the words loudly, importantly, "helps us keep the loft in order. Do we?"

Jennifer's parents looked a bit confused. Her mother replied, "Oh, no. Of course not. Rob's welcome any time."

"Yes, I'm going to speak to Fogarty next egg delivery. Any bets I make him change his mind?"

91.

"Never knew a more persuasive individual, Bertha," her father chuckled. "You'll win on sheer stubbornness."

It was Rob's turn to wonder. He stared at Bertha in surprise. A smile started at the corners of his lips, widening, as Bertha winked, smiling back. Jennifer wanted to hug Aunt Bertha on the spot.

Bertha fingered another Oatmeal Supreme. "Any bets on whether I can resist eating this?" She laughed good-naturedly. "I declare, one of these days I may turn into a blimp!"

Rob sputtered cooky crumbs. Jennifer spit a spray of milk, trying to control the laughing; for no good reason, she giggled harder. Rob tried, too, looking down intently at the plate of Bertha's cookies. He burst into a string of ha-ha-heee-ha-hee-ha-has. And Jennifer, not quite knowing why, laughed even more wildly at that.

The grown-ups didn't understand at all; it seemed like a lot of craziness over nothing much to them. But later, long after Rob had gone home and the family had retreated to bed, Jennifer remembered the warm laughter and giggled into her pillow. She smiled herself to sleep.

It was still dark when Jennifer awoke the following morning. Careful not to wake Bertha or her mother or father, she fumbled for her jeans and shirt in the darkness. She creaked up the stairs to brush her teeth. By the time she had tiptoed from the house and run to the aspen, the larks and jays and swallows had begun welcoming the morning. The world was a music box;

all around her issued the tinkling, high-pitched song of every bird, asking the sun to visit the world for another day. Jennifer was glad to be back.

By the time she had climbed the ladder, the sun had showered touches of gold on the leaves. It filled the loft with a sleepy light. It fell on the tarnished metal of a feeder, the red and blue rims of nesting bowls, and the heads of waking pigeons.

Jennifer seated herself on a bale, drinking in the color. The bowls rested in the orange crates and in the pockets in the hay. On a few of the rims, birds balanced. From a box of cotton tufts and straw and string, some were already sifting for pieces to take to their nests. A few early birds bobbed their beaks through the bars of a feeder for morsels of grain. Others, at a water trough, sucked the clear water thirstily. Some of the birds sighted Jennifer and greeted her with grunts and coos.

Burma, however, was tucked deeper into her bowl. She did not raise her head to Jennifer. She seemed lost and lonely in the bustle of work around her.

"I've brought a book, Burma," she told the bird. "You might say it's a baby book, but I'm going to read it anyway."

Jennifer sat on the floor, away from the busy pigeons, closer to Burma. Perhaps there was, after all, a chance Burma would understand the story that Jennifer read— the words about Patrick, stopping to visit, to stay with a friend, and then moving on home.

" 'Flying home to supper one night, Patrick Pigeon got lost,' " she read. Burma blinked.

She read the whole story, wanting Burma to understand. There was still hope. There was a chance that Homer, too, had only paused to greet a friend.

" 'Patrick knew he must leave the party. His family was waiting at home in another loft,' " Jennifer read.

She glanced at Burma hunched over the bowl.

" 'Patrick Pigeon flew home, at last. He was happy to be in the place he loved best.' "

Jennifer smoothed Burma's feathers. She wondered if Burma even felt the fingers sliding along her back. Perhaps, wrapped in the waiting, she had forgotten to feel.

"I love you, Burma. Please don't be sad."

Burma ruffled her wings and wobbled to the feeder. She pecked at the grain, then returned to the Burma bowl.

It was warm and quiet and safe in the hay. The book tumbled from Jennifer's hands as her eyes closed and she dozed in the sunlight. Jennifer barely heard the distant hum of Ernie's cycle from her place in the loft. Dreaming of the motorcycle, she slept on. As the cycle neared the barn, Jennifer rode the dream-machine, gliding from the road into the air and over the barn roof, feeling the whir of the cycle carrying her to the sun.

11.

She awoke with a start, surprised to be aboard a scratchy bale of hay and not the dream machine. The sound of a voice beyond the barn startled her. She peeked from the loft door.

Rob had yelled a goodbye to Ernie, speeding away

along the road. Now he raced for the barn. She hurried to the ladder and waited for him to appear.

"The loft looks great," she shouted down to him. "It's perfect!"

"Not till we get the netting and build a fly pen outside," Rob said.

He climbed up the ladder, carrying a water bucket. Moving to the loft doorway, he looked around the golden loft. He smiled down at the birds breakfasting at the feeder, then stirred the grain with a finger.

"It's a special mix. Some corn, a bit of peas, kafir, and some hard wheat. I buy it ready-mixed but Oscar used to mix it himself."

He lifted the pail he had carried up the ladder and poured the water into the trough. Cool and foaming, it splashed the drinking pigeons. They shook their feathers, flicking off water.

Rob's pride in the loft shone in his eyes. He inspected each nesting bowl, careful not to disturb the pigeons. A few prodded and pecked at their nests. He checked the progress on the last nest in a row. Then Rob sat down next to Jennifer on the straw.

"Ready to learn their names?"

Jennifer was ready. She had already overheard bits and pieces of pigeon chatter as some of the mothers-to-be tried out baby names for size.

"Proo-dence, Proo-dence," one said to her mate.

He answered by bobbing his head and pecking a piece of yarn into place.

"Trudy, try Trudy," cooed another. Her mate disagreed.

95.

"Hank, Hank," he grunted.

"Oscar named them all long before I met him," Rob said.

Jennifer pulled the tablet from the shoebox.

"The one on the top, over in the corner, is Leyden. Oscar named Leyden after a bird who saved a whole village of people."

"I remember the story about Leyden. In a book I read in the library, I found out about a lot of famous pigeons."

"I bet Oscar told me about all of those. Oscar's better than a book any day."

Jennifer printed in large letters the name of the pigeon, Leyden. "Maybe. But one of these days I'm going to get a bunch of pigeon books. I'm going to learn everything there is to know about pigeons."

Jennifer fastened the slip of paper to the hay near Leyden's perch. She looked closely at Leyden, noting the ring around the neck, the dark markings on the feathers, the shiny band on the leg.

"Most of 'em have a number and a name. Their racing numbers are on the bands." Rob gave her the other names, lots of them namesakes, and she made a name tag for each to help her remember.

"Who was Homer named after?" she asked him.

"Homer was just Homer. He was special enough without a famous name."

Rob looked toward Burma. "You're a queen, Burma. Burma Queen."

Burma did not lift her head. She sat unmoving.

96.

And Rob did not take her from the nest. Jennifer guessed, too, that Burma no longer cared for a gentle hand to soothe her.

"Burma is feeling like Oscar did." Rob's voice was husky. "Oscar got old and tired of waiting. He slept a lot, or he sat in his attic and watched the loft."

Jennifer thought of the note in the attic window.

"He was lonely. He was remembering."

Jennifer spoke. "Remembering what?"

Rob said, "Remembering his sons. They all grew up and moved away to different cities. Once Oscar showed me the places on a map."

Jennifer knew the wonder of cities, but she was sorry the sons had left Oscar.

Rob said, "When Oscar's sons were little, they had the loft and the pigeons . . . and Oscar had them. He thought they'd come back. He kept the pigeons and waited."

Rob rolled onto his back and looked into the rafters. He talked to the rafters, as if Jennifer had gone. "We were both waiting, Oscar and me."

Jennifer wondered if Rob had reminded Oscar of one of his sons. Rob kicked the wall of hay with his foot.

"Oscar got sick. He was sick from the waiting." Rob put a hand over his eyes, as if to shield them from the sun. Silently, he rose and moved to the ladder, climbing down out of sight without another word.

Jennifer wished he had not gone. She felt lonely for Burma's sake and lonely for Rob's as she watched the summer sun rise higher and higher in the sky. She wanted to comfort Burma. She wanted to stop the pain of waiting. Jennifer had never waited very long for anything. But she knew how it felt to be lonely.

"Could someone die of loneliness?" she wondered.

She moved to seek out her secret room and her mother's voice came on the wind into the loft. "Jennifer! Jen! Where are you?"

There was worry in her voice and a little fear. Jennifer had forgotten that she had told no one of her early leaving. She scurried to the ladder and hurried down.

"Jennifer! Come home!"

Jennifer ran, knowing her mother would be glad to know she was safe. Jennifer was glad her mother was near.

We were both waiting, Oscar and me.

Rob's words were with her as she ran. She knew he had been waiting for his mother as well as for Homer, and she ran faster, hoping to leave the loneliness behind her.

12.

There were days to think about Rob's loneliness and days to be lonely herself, waiting in the loft for Rob to appear. More than a week passed with no sign of him.

The eggman had come and gone; a Saturday ago, he

had come and had lingered over coffee, listening to Bertha plead her case for a rascal. From her place in the loft Jennifer had scanned the back of the pickup, the stand of aspen, the meadows that stretched to town, sure that the rascal would come, but he hadn't.

The eggman had gone. She had watched the truck follow the dusty road to town; she had seen Bertha wave from the porch. Later, Bertha assured them that there was nothing to keep Rob from the loft, now that Fogarty had had her brand of persuading.

That Rob had not appeared, not even since the egg-man's visit, had escaped Bertha, her mind on going home. Evenings, she had taken to sitting on the swing, squeaking creaking, addressing her thoughts to the dark.

"Remodeling—who needs it? They probably botched up the job. How long does it take to put in new plumbing anyway?"

There had been no message to advise her that the apartment was ready, but the day came when Bertha decided to return anyway.

"I'm tired," she had said, "of a suitcase life."

Bertha had departed, hours before, on the Saturday bus to the city. And Jennifer had missed her chance to ask the eggman what had become of Rob.

Now, alone in the loft, she poured the feed and the water for the birds, as she had done every day of the waiting. She swept the loft floor another time and listened to the pigeon chatter. Busy with their own housekeeping, they ignored her. She moved to the door-way where she and Burma had daily watched the sky for a glimpse of wings in the empty blue. She had studied the fields for a flash of Rob's windbreaker, too. She had seen neither.

For days the sky had held nothing but sun; it had scorched away the clouds. Only in the evenings, when the mountain breezes glided into the dark valley, had relief come. Today the air had a burden of waiting in it. Swirls of dirt rose from the parched fields and the land held a film of dust. Jennifer could wait no longer.

She found herself crossing the meadow to the road that led to Del Norte where Rob lived. Scuffling over gravel and earth, she breathed in the dust of rainless days.

She reached the town thirsty and sticky with sweat. Anxious to find Rob, she did not pause to rest. She had decided that Mrs. Priebe's store was as good a place as any to begin searching. As she walked in, the bell over the door jangled.

Two girls turned from the magazine rack to stare at Jennifer. They were Jennifer's size, perhaps eleven or twelve. One of them whispered into her friend's ear. The other girl giggled.

Jennifer spied the salami-and-cheese lady, stacking dog food.

"Hello, Mrs. Priebe." The words came out as a whisper. Jennifer had not expected to be nervous.

"Why, it's Jennifer. Nice to see you, dear."

Behind their comic books, the two girls whispered to each other.

"I'm looking for Mr. Fogarty's house. Could you tell me where he lives?"

100.

Mrs. Priebe's eyes widened. "The eggman's place? If it's eggs you want, we've got some here in the store. Fresh as Mr. Fogarty's, mind you, and just as cheap."

"I'm not looking for eggs. I'm looking for Robert Fogarty."

Mrs. Priebe frowned. "If that's the case, you're looking for trouble." She looked back to the two girls. "Pamela and Nina will tell you as much."

Pamela and Nina left the comic books and joined Mrs. Priebe.

"He's a bully. Isn't that so, Nina?" Pamela narrowed her eyes into two slits.

She looked as ugly as anyone Jennifer had ever seen. Nina only looked fearful—and dumb.

"That's so," echoed Nina.

Pamela went on. "He makes trouble at school. He pulls my hair whenever he gets a chance."

Jennifer felt like pulling Pamela's hair herself.

"He's so mean, he cooped up a pigeon in a truck and sent it off to Oregon. Pure meanness made him do it," Pamela poked Nina.

"That's right," said Nina.

Jennifer knew the bird was Homer.

Mrs. Priebe patted Jennifer on the head. "He's a bad apple. You mix with him and you mix with trouble."

"Maybe you haven't tried to be friendly," Jennifer said.

"He doesn't make friends easy," said Mrs. Priebe. "Person he liked best was Oscar Olson, the old man who used to live at your place."

"And he likes the tough boys at school, like his

101.

brothers. The ones who hate the teachers and the girls."

"That's right," said Nina.

"He likes me," Jennifer said.

She didn't care what they thought of her. She didn't care if Pamela told everybody in town that she was the friend of a troublemaker. Pamela and Nina and Mrs. Priebe looked suprised.

"I'm Rob's friend and I'm not sorry. I'm proud."

Jennifer walked to the door and out onto Grand Street. She felt a knot forming in her stomach. She moved without thinking, following the street to the end of the line of stores and houses, forgetting to ask directions. She turned at a street marked Clayton and walked on until she reached another, Grove. She seemed to be going nowhere. The knot stayed with her. There was no guarantee, she knew, that she would find Rob even if she covered all the streets in the little town. No matter. She would walk them two times, three times if she had to.

She turned another corner. Only yards away, Ernie sat tinkering with his motorcycle. With him were two other older boys bending over the engine. They paid no attention to Jennifer. Only Ernie noticed her. His eyes smiled a silent greeting. He tipped his head toward a house nearby.

Jennifer skirted the clutter of wrenches and bolts on the sidewalk. The two boys, who reminded her of Rob, were his brothers, she guessed; she was glad they had not noticed her. She walked quietly to the house.

It was, indeed, the eggman's place with a yard full of

coops of cackling hens. The back door was open. Jennifer peered through the screen into the dark kitchen. Rob stood at the stove, frying eggs. He looked small by the big stove, and lonely. Jennifer felt his loneliness. She coughed to let him know that she had come.

Rob looked up. He said nothing. Jennifer watched him set down the spatula and turn off the burner. He was more a shadow than a boy in the dark kitchen. He left the eggs and came to the door.

"Hi," she said.

"Hi."

She wondered what to say next. Away from the loft, he seemed like a stranger. He stood quietly, his face crisscrossed with screening.

"We're still waiting, Burma and me," she said.

"Good for you."

His voice tried to be tough. But Jennifer heard the sadness in it. He gave the screen door a push and slipped through the crack.

"My ma's coming to visit. I can go with her to the city to live if I want to."

The news surprised her. Jennifer wanted to ask him to stay.

"I'm sorry you'll be leaving," she told him.

Rob sat on the doorstep. He cracked his knuckles as he stared at the ground.

"I haven't decided yet. It would be good to leave behind the crummy school and stuff."

He paused.

"It would be better if my ma came back here."

Jennifer sat on the grass and looked up at Rob. He had a faraway look in his eyes.

"Might she decide to come back, to stay?"

"I used to think so. But I was pretending."

Jennifer wished she could help Rob. There was nothing she could say. She waited for him to speak.

"I was pretending about Homer, too. Do you know what happened to Homer?"

Jennifer shook her head.

"Some hawk probably ripped him apart. They eat pigeons, ya know. Or Homer rammed himself into a building . . . that can happen if a bird flies in the fog. Or hunters shot him and cooked him for supper. Or Homer got lost in the mountains. He got lost and died."

"Those are lies!" Jennifer shouted.

She held back the tears. She hated Rob for giving up. She hated him for hurting her.

Rob wasn't sorry. "It's true," he said. "It was dumb to think he'd come back. I was pretending things would work out. Things never do."

He stood up. Jennifer watched him return to the darkness, slamming the screen door behind him.

"You just wait!" she blurted out. "Homer'll come back—you'll see!"

She turned and raced from the yard, past the brothers returning home, and down Willow. Ernie was waiting at the corner. He surprised Jennifer by signaling for her to come over.

"How are the birds doing?"

106.

Jennifer tried not to show the hurt. She forgot Ernie's question and asked one of her own.

"Why did he have to send Homer away in the first place?"

Ernie drummed his fingers on the motorcycle seat. He spoke softly when he answered her. "He did it for a friend, out of love. Homer was a gift and nobody sees that."

Jennifer listened, remembering Rob's sadness.

"Oscar's son sent for the furniture, a few weeks after he took Oscar to live with him. Rob figured the movers would find the bird when they unloaded the truck, figured Oscar would get the bird and maybe get well. Nobody else figured the same. They called Rob a dummy for sending Homer away."

Jennifer's hurt was for Rob now. "Maybe they never found the bird," she said.

Ernie sighed. "That's what Rob's pa thought. He wanted Rob to forget about the bird. To stop moping around your place, thinking about Oscar." Ernie paused. "Rob's pa figured the old man died before Homer reached him."

Jennifer wouldn't let herself believe it.

"Will you deliver a message for me, Ernie?"

Ernie looked at her curiously. "I guess so."

Jennifer hopped on the back of the cycle. "To Mrs. Priebe's store, Ernest!"

Ernie revved the cycle and drove to Grand Street. They passed Pamela and Nina. The girls stood wide-eyed in amazement as Jennifer raced by them on the

107.

back of bashful Ernie's cycle. Ernie pulled up at the curb in front of the store.

"I'll be out in a minute!" Jennifer said.

She ran to the counter and pulled some change from her pocket.

"A tablet and a pencil, please." Jennifer smiled her widest smile at Mrs. Priebe.

Jennifer did not wait for a bag. She was out on the curb in a flash, scribbling her map and a message. She guessed that Mrs. Priebe was peeking down at her from behind the displays in the window. Guarding her message, Jennifer bent over the paper.

She quickly sketched the map of the loft. She drew arrows from the ladder to the tunnel and the secret room.

She wrote beneath the map:
TRY SECRET ROOM.

She reread the message and added another sentence:
FLASH—LOFT HAS MAGIC!
HOMER WILL RETURN!

She folded it and pushed the note into Ernie's hand. He knew, without asking, who it was for.

"Crazy kid," he mumbled beneath the motorcycle roar.

"Thanks, Ernie," Jennifer shouted.

She whirled around and waved to Mrs. Priebe, who was indeed peering over a pile of canteloupes. Mrs. Priebe blushed and waved a little wave.

Jennifer turned a cartwheel and headed home.

108.

13.

Having reclaimed the right to sleep upstairs, Jennifer crawled beneath the quilt of her own cozy bed. She felt safe beneath the old comforter, and thought of autumn mornings and cold wooden floors beneath bare feet when the days would be as crisp as these Colorado nights.

Soon school would begin. Soon, as the winds chilled and the leaves crackled yellow, pigeon babies would grow up in the loft. She gazed up at the ceiling and thought of first snow, of how it might hug the aspen and the fence posts, come winter. She would make a hundred snow angels. Her angels would stretch around the loft and into town and up to Rob's door. Jennifer slept. Jennifer dreamed of a gigantic egg hovering above her in the sky, a wonder she wanted to share with a boy who hid somewhere in the shadows.

"Crash!"

Jennifer sat up, jolted from the dream.

"Crash!"

She fully awoke as a second flash lighted up the quilt and the flapping curtains. Lightning raced ahead of thunder, streaking the sky with ghostly white.

The rain had come and, with it, the angry wind. Jennifer shivered. She pulled the quilt above her head, feeling the wind at her toes before she pulled them beneath the cover. Through the window, the rain rushed in on the wind. It drenched the sill.

Footsteps pattered along the hall. Jennifer's mother moved quickly to the window to shut it. Now the wind rattled the pane, whining to get in. The rain clattered at the glass. But they were safe and dry and together in the warm pocket of the house. Jennifer whispered, "Thank you."

"Back to sleep, love," her mother whispered back.

She kissed Jennifer on the forehead and tucked the quilt tightly around her, wrapping her in a soft cocoon. Jennifer listened to her mother's footsteps until they padded away to bed. She snuggled deeper into her cocoon.

Lightning pierced the sky, tearing away the darkness. Thunder boomed as close as the old barn. Jennifer shut her eyes. Tucking her head close to her chest, she remembered Burma.

Letting out a little cry, Jennifer sat up in the darkness. Jennifer imagined the loft door standing open to the storm and Burma being lashed by the wind and rain.

"She'll move. She'll find a warm place to hide," Jennifer told herself.

She remembered Burma's loneliness. Burma had waited too long. She had grown tired of waiting. Her head tucked deep into her breast, her wings folded, she would give in to the storm.

110.

Jennifer arose in the darkness and felt her way to the window. She saw the aspen bending in the wind. The road swirled with mud. A shirt left hanging on the line flapped crazily, struggling to escape.

Burma was Rob's bird. But he had given up waiting; he had deserted her. He would not care that now she was in danger.

"If Burma gets sick, it will serve him right. Rob doesn't care what happens," Jennifer thought.

Jennifer thought again. She knew Rob would care. She guessed that it had been fear that had kept him from the loft. He had been afraid to keep waiting and hoping.

Jennifer slipped into her sneakers. She felt for her jeans and slipped into them. Tucking her pajama top into her jeans and pulling the quilt over her head, she moved warily down the stairs. She felt her way across the dark living room to the door. The comforter tugged at her shoulders. She gathered it around her body and turned the doorknob.

A gust of wind opened the door. Jennifer slipped outside, shutting the door carefully, soundlessly.

Rain pelted the porch. Wind whipped at Jennifer's hair. She clasped the quilt tighter and felt the cold rain against her face. Lightning knifed through the clouds. Moments later, thunder crashed against the night sky. It made Jennifer jump. She huddled against the doorway. Another streak lighted the way to the aspen, but Jennifer was afraid to follow.

Trembling under the quilt, she stared at the emptiness between the porch and the trees. She knew the light-

111.

ning could strike her down if she ran through the open space to the aspen. It might seek her out in the trees . . . it could find her in the field of corn. Or it might claim her as she raced the last stretch up the slope to the barn.

Yet, Burma trembled in the loft. Burma needed a friend. And Rob needed Burma, Jennifer knew.

Jennifer dashed from the porch. She found herself in the downpour, the mud spattering her feet and legs. Running, never stopping, she raced toward the aspen.

She tried to run faster but the quilt pulled her back. The ground beneath her feet turned to pools of sucking sand and mud. Head down, clinging to the quilt, she pushed ahead.

The trees! She had reached the trees! But the rain fell through the leaves and branches. It slapped at her face. It pelted the quilt, soaking it with more water, pulling Jennifer down with it.

She found a path between the trees and ran. The quilt rode her back like a heavy animal, pressing down on her. Jennifer's muscles strained under the burden, but she kept running, bringing the cover with her.

Rumble-thunder-crash! The lightning split through the trees and Jennifer froze in her fear. She grasped the trunk of an aspen. She told herself to run. Run-Jennifer-run. The cornstalks were wet, slimy against her skin. She moved through the corn, pushing against the rain and the cold. At the edge of the field she peered toward the barn, the yawn in the wall, the place where Burma waited.

She forgot the cold. She thought of the loft and

grew impatient to be there, cradling the Christmas-card bird in her hands.

Jennifer pulled at the quilt. It was sluggish with rain-water; the edges dragged in the mud. The coldness of it made Jennifer shiver. She shook it off her shoulders. Leaving it behind her in the mud, she picked up speed. Forgetting her fears, Jennifer ran ahead, her mind and her heart on Burma.

14.

"*One—*"

Jennifer began the count. Each time her foot touched the next rung, she counted.

"Two—three—"

Jennifer stared ahead into darkness as she climbed. Fear climbed with her as it had the first time she had moved up the rickety ladder.

"Four—five—six—"

Blackness filled the barn and Jennifer ached to be home.

"Seven—"

The ladder creaked. Jennifer froze in her place. She held her breath and waited for the sound of footsteps—perhaps of a stranger who now hid in the barn from the thunder and from her.

Jennifer gripped the ladder, not moving. The creaking echoed in her mind. From her head, drips of rain plunked to her shoulders, skimmed her neck, spattered from her arms.

Jennifer took a deep breath. She climbed higher.

"Eight-nine-ten-eleven!"

Creak, crick, creak.

A lightning streak filled the loft with an eerie light. Then, rumbling, came the thunder.

"Twelve. Thirteen."

The old ladder creaked again. Jennifer steadied herself and whispered a plea to the ladder.

"Don't break now. Don't!"

Jennifer wondered why she had not had the sense to stay home. Yet, she climbed.

"Fourteen—

"Fifteen—

"Sixteen."

"I'll make it. I'll make it." Jennifer was her own cheering section.

She forgot about the count; now she knew the top rungs without counting. She felt the one bowed in the middle. She waited for the creak, as always, on the next. Her foot touched the nail head jutting from the next rung, and she knew, without seeing, the place of the last.

Up one more, scamper, scramble, up and over. Jennifer curled into a little ball on the loft floor. A hotness rushed through her. Her heart pounded. The darkness swirled around her.

Yet, familiar smells brought comfort . . . the sweetness of hay and pigeon feathers. It was warm in the loft, warmest near the walls of hay. She moved around the corner of hay to join the pigeons.

Burma hunched over the nest, the one Rob had made for her. Rain drove in sheets through the loft opening.

Jennifer hurried to the opening, feeling the force of the rain on her cheeks and shoulders. Reaching toward the tiny shape that was Burma, Jennifer patted the raindrops from the bird's head and back. Burma was a shadow in the storm. Jennifer soothed her.

"Rest, Burma, poor Burma."

The other birds huddled on their perches in the hay. The thunder rolled along the roofbeams, and the pigeons' complaints—grunts and whistles—drowned beneath the rumble.

Jennifer reached for the rope handle of the loft door. Tugging the heavy door toward her, she shut out the rain and closed in the darkness. Through the crack, a slice of sky flashed silver with every streak of lightning.

Groping for the shoebox, Jennifer took out the music box and wound it. She lifted Burma and hugged the bird to her.

The single notes of the music box tinkled one by one into the darkness, playing a thin tune below and between the roar of the storm. The song from the music box could not fill the space of the loft. Jennifer felt like the timid notes, too weak against the night and the storm. Alone, guarding the birds from the wind, Jennifer felt she might never get home again. Home seemed farther away than the trees and the night, much farther.

"The storm will be over soon," she assured the pigeons. "Don't be afraid."

Across the emptiness, the birds answered Jennifer. The music slowed to a last tinkling note, then nothing.

115.

The birds and Jennifer listened in the new quiet. Already the thunder sounded farther away, moving to the mountains and taking the lightning with it.

Bang! The barn door slammed shut. Below her, footsteps crunched across the floor. Someone was coming. As Jennifer listened, fear dried her mouth and made her tremble.

The first rung of the ladder creaked in the darkness.

She wanted the stranger to be Rob, come the three miles from town through the storm to comfort the birds, especially Burma. Who else would seek out the loft? A hobo, perhaps, needing safety from the storm? A criminal hiding from the law? How about Henry Thatcher, Jennifer thought, somebody as crazy as a Henry Thatcher in the attic, who had seen her heading for the loft and was coming to kill her?

Whoever climbed the ladder would hear her if she ran for her secret room. Whoever came climbed quickly, creaking noisily. She crouched lower in the corner, bending over Burma.

Jennifer's father would have called out to her, she knew. This intruder was silent. Only the ladder talked of his coming. Then a shuffle at the ledge. Around the corner of hay, a shape appeared in the darkness. For a moment, Jennifer's heart seemed to stop beating. She watched the shadowy form move toward her, coming closer and closer.

Lightning filled the room with whiteness, piercing through the crack in the door. Jennifer started. Not an arm's length from her, the intruder stared with bulging eyes at her frightened face.

Thunder boomed. Blackness returned. Jennifer recalled the intruder's surprised face. He panted, catching his breath. Jennifer calmed herself. Now his voice filled the room.

"What are you doing here?"

"Me?" Jennifer said. "How did you get here?"

"I ran."

"You're crazy!"

"I guess I am," he said.

Jennifer felt him grinning in the darkness. "Rob, I'm glad you're here. I was getting the creeps alone."

Jennifer tried to hide her surprise. His coming through the storm, all the way from town, had surprised her, but not his love for Burma.

Rob flicked on a flashlight and lighted a corner of the loft. He had carried a sack of supplies on his back from town. He laid the pack between them and pulled out a woolen muffler, then a canteen. Next to them he laid a dry flannel shirt. Finally, he reached in and brought forth a can opener and three cans of beans.

Jennifer chuckled. "Boy, you're sure planning on staying here a lot longer than I am!"

"Aw, I just wanted to be prepared," he said.

Rob crawled closer. "Is Burma okay? I figured you'd take care of her."

Jennifer wanted to turn a cartwheel. She wanted to sing alleluias. She only put Burma back on her bowl.

"She seems okay. I got the water off her."

Rob crawled over to the bowl. He pulled the wet winter cap from the bowl and replaced it with the warm muffler.

"Burma girl, we'll keep you warm," he said.

Jennifer thought of the old man, Oscar. She knew he would be glad to know that Rob still loved his birds. She hoped Homer had let him know.

The light of the flashlight gave a weak glow as Rob placed Burma in the bowl and moved to check on the other pigeons. They were restless, complaining about the storm and the late-night visitors, but safe.

"Here, Jennifer."

He held out the flannel shirt. Jennifer felt the cold mud caking on her feet and legs. Her clothes, drenched with rain, drooped. She looked more closely at Rob now as he wrung the water from his windbreaker. He, too, was dripping wet. His shoes were covered with mud.

Jennifer smiled in the darkness. She put on the shirt. It warmed her.

"Better wait for the rain to stop before we head home," he said.

"If I get back early enough, nobody will guess I've been gone," Jennifer said.

He skimmed a glob of mud off of Jennifer's sneakers. He held a fingerful in front of her nose.

"Nobody will guess?"

Jennifer laughed. She did not care about morning. She was glad to be here with her friend.

120.

"When my pa told me I could start coming here again, I don't think he meant in the middle of the night."

Jennifer teased him. "If he's too mad to let you come home, you can stay here and live on beans!"

"That's what I figured." He was serious, turning a can in his hands. "I promised I'd try not to make as much trouble for him any more. I promised I'd mind him better."

"Oh, he'll understand! I'll stick up for you. You had to come for Burma."

Rob looked at Jennifer. "If it hadn't been for you, Jennifer, I'd have given up."

He tucked the cans into the sack, smiling.

"Today I told my pa that I'd decided. I told him I was staying in Del Norte with him."

He looked up sheepishly. "You should've seen him. He hooted out loud when I told him, and hugged me. I didn't know I could make him so happy, just by sticking around!"

Jennifer felt a warm excitement tingling through her, making her want to cheer as Rob's father had done.

"I miss my ma, but if I moved to the city, I'd miss my pa. And I'd miss this place. It's where I belong."

Rob pulled a map, the one Jennifer had drawn, from the sack. He studied it by the flashlight glow, pacing toward the opposite wall, around the corner of hay, to the secret room. Jennifer was glad to share the secret with her friend.

She smelled the rain-air, and through the crack in the

121.

door watched a single star peep from behind the clouds. The angry storm, only a grumble now, had rolled into the mountains. She settled back against the hay and waited for Rob to return.

At last he did. He crept quietly back to Burma's nest.

"It's a good place," he said.

Jennifer blinked. She had almost fallen asleep.

". . . for being alone in," she added.

"I thought about Oscar there. I miss him."

Rob nudged the loft door, pushing it out to the sky and a drizzle of rain. Rob put his head on his knees.

"I think Oscar died."

The clouds moved beyond the aspen. The stars showed one by one. The thunder rumbled far away. And still Jennifer did not know how to answer.

"He won't be back, ever," Rob said.

Jennifer said, "The birds are here. Oscar's birds."

She knew the words did not ease the hurt.

"Oscar's birds and mine."

Rob thought about his words. ". . . and yours, Jennifer," he said.

Jennifer nodded. They watched Burma, wrapped in the muffler. Jennifer knew that part of Oscar was with the birds. And Rob had Oscar in his heart, just as Gerard and Lisa and Gilpin Street were in hers.

Rob fell asleep. He lay next to Burma, one hand over her wings. Not wanting to waken him, Jennifer closed the loft door against the chill and then moved to her secret room.

She had only meant to linger there a minute or two,

122.

but she was tired. The rain-music and the sweet hay wrapped her in a fog of sleep.

She curved herself into a corner of hay and closed her eyes, thankful for thunder and Burma and adventures, before she fell asleep.

15.

A mystery tapped at the window of the secret room. Jennifer tightened in sleep, dreaming of a magician who shuffled his cards on the steps of Mrs. Priebe's store.

The mystery would not be gone. Above her, it flap-flapped like a shuffled deck. She wished for a pillow to cushion her head, to take away the sound.

The sound remained, flap-flapping, whooshing. She awoke to a thump on the roof.

Jennifer lay in the secret room, listening. In the silence, she imagined stars and wisps of leftover drizzle and a crescent Christmas cooky moon.

Again she heard the strange shuffle, the flap-flapping on the roof. Jennifer could guess a reason for the sound, but she was afraid to believe it. Her head whirled, filled to bursting with a name she dared not say. She fumbled for the window latch. Letting the window swing open, she pushed into the sky and searched the darkness.

On the peak of the roof, huddled against the stars, was a bird. He looked small and beaten. Never mind that he trembled, barely alive. She knew the magic bird. Homer had come home.

"Homer," she called gently.

The bird raised his head.

Jennifer felt the tears well up, blurring her sight. She laughed through the blur. Leaning out the window, she held out her hand to the bird.

"Homer, come home."

The bird cocked his head, looking at Jennifer. He seemed to hesitate, not knowing whether to heed the strange girl's welcome. He clung to the rooftop, sidling toward her, then wobbling back.

She decided to awaken Rob. Homer would know him and come. She retreated into the little room. As she moved, Homer moved too.

He came feebly, flapping a tattered wing, thumping on the shingles, across the eaves, fluttering onto the window ledge.

Jennifer held her breath, afraid to call out to Rob, afraid of frightening Homer away from the window. She waited for Homer to move into the room, but he wobbled on the ledge, too weak or too hurt to try. Jennifer felt wonder and fear for the broken bird. Hardly believing, she touched a single finger to his head, down the neck and over his back. Homer had become a wish. Now, like magic, the wish had become a bird in the loft with her and Rob and Burma.

Homer trembled. Jennifer soothed him, brushing her fingers along his head and his back. Her fingers felt lightly over wetness and blood and battered feathers, careful not to hurt him more.

She slipped her fingers between Homer's feet, letting him rest on her forearm. In the darkness, Homer pecked

124.

at the hand that held him. He tried halfheartedly to break from her hold. Homer's round eyes blinked back at her in the blackness. He was proud, even in this beaten way.

"I'll take you to the loft floor," she whispered. "To Rob and to Burma."

She covered his wings and back with her free hand, heading for the tunnel. Inching along on her belly, she cradled Homer in her hands and the tired bird rode the darkness, not needing to fly any farther. He did not fight her hold any longer. He was weary and he was hurt. Jennifer worked her way to the wooden floor and hurried around the wall of hay, carrying Homer.

Rob lay against the hay, Burma beneath his hand. Jennifer wondered how to tell him—whether to shout the news or to wake him gently, out of a dream.

Burma knew. She fluttered and flapped her stiff wings, hurrying to her mate. She spread her wings and greeted Homer, bobbing and cooing a love hello in pigeon language.

The motion startled Rob from sleep. He blinked awake to find Jennifer kneeling before him, and Homer between them. Confused, Rob peered closer at the bird, ·then up at Jennifer.

"It's Homer," she cried. "He's here, Rob!"

Rob crept to Homer and touched a cheek to Homer's wings. Homer cooed to Burma and to Rob and Jennifer a low and weary greeting. Rob's eyes shone with tears. He was happy Homer was home, Jennifer knew, but he cried.

She waited and watched for sunlight. She would

125.

have time to tell Rob how she had discovered Homer on the roof. She would show him, too, the note in the attic, Oscar's note that had led her to the loft.

Suddenly Rob darted to the ladder and disappeared. Jennifer heard a clatter of tin and wire, wood and gravel, above the noises of the now talkative pigeon family. She listened to the rush of water spurting from the spigot. Back again, Rob carried a carton into the loft.

"The birds sometimes get riled over a wounded one," he explained. "This box'll keep Homer safe until he gets better."

Out of the carton he pulled a patch of chicken wire and a dampened cloth. Quickly Jennifer took off the flannel shirt, rolling it into a soft cushion for Homer.

Rob gripped Homer firmly, dabbing lovingly at the wounds with the wet rag. Homer's body was matted with blood. There were gashes and cuts on his head and along one side of his body.

"We can wait till sunup to take him to the vet. He's going to be all right, Jennifer."

She saw it first, the note tucked into the numbered band. Rob saw it then, as he placed Homer in the box, and pulled the paper from the band on Homer's leg, hastening then to place the mesh over the carton.

Quickly he unfolded the paper and read the message. Jennifer read it too.

HOMER BROUGHT MAGIC
OF LOFT TO ME. I SEND HIM BACK
WITH LOVE. HOMER TO BURMA,
OVER AND OUT. OSCAR

126.

"Oscar—all the way from Oregon!" Rob mumbled.

And Jennifer thought of the magic words: with love, with love, with love.

Rob read the message again and again, glancing often at Homer in the box, as if he weren't sure the bird would be there when he looked next.

"Sunup soon," Jennifer guessed. "I'll have to be going then."

"I'll go back to the house with you, Jennifer."

Jennifer knew it would not be easy for Rob to come along. It was the kind of favor only a friend would do.

"Thanks, Rob," she said. She smiled, thinking that he looked happier than she had ever seen him.

Rob and Jennifer waited for a new day, the loft more special than it had ever been.

Jennifer hummed a forgotten lullaby to the family of birds.

"Shoo, shoo, shoo la ru. . . . Shoo la rack shack, shoola boppa coo."

The first rays of the sun crept over the mountains, bringing a rosy tinge to the sky and filling the loft with light.

Rising to go, Jennifer cooed to Burma, "Peace, Burma, peace."

And the sun sparkled in, lighting roofbeams and feathers and the faces of friends.

127.